TWO LOVERS ARE ALWAYS BETTER
THAN ONE...

"I told you I would get it for you." Randy's voice was filled with amusement. He always seemed happy, even though Sean knew better. The dark secrets of Randy's years in the SEALS were well hidden from most, but Sean knew them.

When he stepped into the kitchen, he blinked. There were bowls everywhere... and flour. It was all over the counter and the floor.

"What the fuck, Jaime?"

She offered him a snarl. "We are not all giants, Sean. You put your flour way up on top."

"I can reach it there."

She settled her hands on her ships and offered him a nasty look. "Well, I can't."

"I only have to worry about myself, so I put it where I want."

Randy chuckled. "You definitely do."

Dammit, he didn't like the way his body responded to Randy's innuendo. That bridge was burned. Sean tossed him a dirty look. "Behave."

"Why? You behave enough for both of us."

A LITTLE HARMLESS REVENGE

HARMLESS, BOOK 11

MELISSA SCHROEDER

HARMLESS PUBLISHING

*Especially for
Liz McChesney*

Copyright © 2017 by Melissa Schroeder, 2nd edition

All rights reserved.

No part of this book may be reproduced in any form or by any electronic or mechanical means, including information storage and retrieval systems, without written permission from the author, except for the use of brief quotations in a book review.

This is a work of fiction and any resemblance to real people or events is strictly an accident.

Edited by Noel Varner

Cover by Scott Walker

ISBN: 978-1-939734-57-0

Print ISBN: 978-1975723330

original title: A Little Harmless Rumor

I

PRELUDE TO A REVENGE

PART ONE

1

As Sean watched Lassiter drone on about the mission, he barely paid attention. Sure, the target was one of the richest men in the world, who just happened to be paranoid as fuck. It didn't matter. He was completely and absolutely entranced by his new partner Jaime Alexander.

He couldn't remember when he had been so damned preoccupied by a woman. Her light brown skin and curvy body would tempt any man, but the intelligent hazel gaze drew Sean more than that. He liked a smart woman. Stupid women tended to get on his nerves, and there was no doubt, this woman would not.

Of course, at the moment, she was reading over the report and ignoring him. That intrigued him even more.

"Kaheaku, you paying attention?"

He looked up at Lassiter. The man was giving Sean a knowing look. Damn. Busted.

"Yes. I understand the job. It isn't like I haven't done it a million times before now."

Lassiter rolled his eyes. "Listen, this is my last job, and I want it to go without a hitch. Do you understand?" He included Jaime in the question. She glanced up and nodded, then looked back to the report.

Lassiter gave Sean his full attention. Sean held his hands out and smiled. "Of course. Just as long as your fellow countrywoman can keep it together."

Jaime glanced over at him. "God save me from men who feel the need to have *measuring* contests."

Instead of getting mad, he chuckled, then looked at Lassiter. "Okay, we won't have any problems."

Lassiter nodded.

"Anything else?" he asked.

"No. The event is formal tonight, so make sure to wear a tux."

He acknowledged that with a nod, and turned to Jaime. "I'll pick you up at eight, is that good?"

She nodded but said nothing, as her attention was back on the report. He left and started down the hall. He didn't always fool around on the job. Truth was, before now, he hadn't been all that interested in his partners—both men and women; Sean had a taste for both. He'd only been a civilian for eighteen months, and he had been in ten operations. He knew that people tended to have intense relationships for very short periods of time. There was always a chance this was the last UC. One mistake and you could end up dead. Still, there was that chance you could die that made a person take romantic chances. And he definitely wanted to take a chance with Ms. Jaime Alexander.

Just thinking her name and he felt slightly light-headed. Jesus, it was like he was fourteen and in love again for the first time. His palms were sweaty just thinking about being with her tonight. She had a saucy British accent, one from the other side of the tracks. Add in her husky voice, which slipped beneath his skin and whispered across his soul, and he was a goner.

He shook his head and drew in a deep breath. He had to keep his brain on the game or they would be in trouble. With new purpose, he walked down the hallway to his room. He had worked a lot of jobs, but this one had more danger than usual. Since they were new partners, Sean knew there would be a few bumps tonight. Hopefully, everything would turn out fine in the end. Bug the office, get out alive, and then, he might just get a taste of the very luscious Jaime Alexander.

∼

"He's as arrogant as I had heard," Jaime said when they were alone.

Lassiter smiled at her. He was an attractive man, always had been, and Jaime had always had a thing for older men. He wasn't that much older, maybe ten years, but he had a way about him. From his tailor made suits, to the touch of gray at his temples, Royce Lassiter was a man who drew a lot of attention. For some reason, though, she had never been attracted to him that way. He was more like an older brother to her.

"He has good reason to be. He's the best recruit we've had in years."

"Walter Hayes trained him."

He nodded and looked out the window. "And Hayes said he was his best student."

Inwardly, she sighed. It wasn't Kaheaku's fault that she was feeling inferior. Lassiter had found her and trained her. She was as good of an agent as Sean, but she did not have his reputation.

She would soon though. Working with him on her way up would definitely help. Keeping up with Kaheaku would give her some points in other agents' eyes. It stung that she had to play the game, but she understood. She was the unknown, the one person no one knew about.

"Just remember, he likes to improvise. He's good at it so follow his lead."

She glanced at him out of the corner of her eye, then picked up her purse. "Don't worry about me, love. I know how to handle myself."

She was almost out of the door when he stopped her with a comment. "This isn't play time tonight, Jaime. Nicolai Letov will not negotiate if you two are discovered."

"I'm sure we'll be able to handle it."

He shook his head. "Just be extra careful. He will get the information from you and then he will kill you."

"You think Kaheaku and I cannot keep our mouths shut."

His lips flatted and he made a sound of disgust. "No. I think both of you could handle it very well—at first. You are both stubborn enough. But, Letov has a particular forte."

"That being?"

"He gets people to talk, and then he gets them to beg him to die. He was trained by some of the best ex-KGB agents around. Just make sure you listen to Sean."

With a smile she knew held very little humor, she said, "Don't worry, sir. I can handle Kaheaku."

With that, she slipped out the door and shut it behind her. When she was alone in her room, she leaned against the door and closed her eyes. She had heard the rumors, knew of the man, but seeing him in person was a bit more than she had expected.

At least six three or four, he towered over her, but he didn't use it against her. She could tell he was a man who used his personality for that. She couldn't fight the smile. She liked arrogant men, and Sean Kaheaku had that in spades. God, he was gorgeous. She closed her eyes and his image materialized.

His inky hair was a tad bit too long, and he had the most amazing green eyes. What she wouldn't give to have his sexy mouth on her flesh. His golden brown skin looked as if it had been kissed by the sun. It had been rainy the last month or so, and she knew he had been in England, which confirmed one thing for her. His skin was that shade from the tips of his toes to the top of his head. Jaime shivered.

She pushed herself away from the door and tried to concentrate on what she needed to do. They had to look like a couple who belonged. It wouldn't be a problem for someone like her. Jaime had been pretending to belong most of her life. Now, at least, she could make a living at it and not end up in prison.

2

Sean straightened his bowtie in the mirror, then checked his cufflinks. The light flashed off the diamonds and he shook his head. It still stunned him that he had ended up where he was before the age of thirty. When he'd left Hawaii with nothing but the clothes on his back and orders to report to basic training, he had thought he would make a career out of the Army. Red tape had frustrated him on too many levels, and when Walter had found him, Sean had been only too glad to leave the military behind. Now, he drove cars that cost more than he had ever earned in one year, and wore clothes tailored to fit.

He rolled his shoulders. He should be happier.

Money does not make a man happy.

He smiled when he heard his mother's voice in his head. Money had never been important to her, but it had become a priority to him. When his stepfather had disowned him, Sean had set out to prove he could make it on his own. Of course, now, he couldn't really tell his family he was working for MI-6—even as a contractor. He had to pretend to be doing something else…but that was okay with him. He hadn't talked to his stepfather since

A LITTLE HARMLESS REVENGE

he'd thrown Sean out of the house. Some people were just never going to accept his bisexuality.

Sean pushed those thoughts aside and grabbed his wallet and car keys. He didn't have time to worry about shit like that. He definitely didn't want to keep Jaime waiting too long.

Just thinking her name brought her back to the forefront of his mind, and he glanced at the connecting door. They had a suite of rooms at the hotel, one that provided them with much of the top floor. It also gave people the idea that they were married, or at least involved. Another glance in the mirror and he frowned. What was wrong with him? He was nervous about her on a level he didn't understand. Maybe it was because he hadn't been with a woman in a long time. He'd been working mainly with men in recent months, and several of them swung his way. Going out and finding a woman would have been a complication he didn't need. But, Fate decided to drop what he saw as the perfect woman for the moment right into his lap.

He walked over to her door and waited for a second, listening. Then, he rolled his shoulders, ordered himself to quit being an ass, and knock on her door. Hell, in a few short hours he had gone from interested into almost obsessive about his partner for the night. It wasn't like him at all, but he had a feeling it had to do with the job at hand. Okay, it had a *lot* to do with the woman, but part of it was the mission. He tended to focus on things outside of the job so that he didn't freak the fuck out. It was one of the games that Walter had taught him.

He smiled. There had been very few positive male role models in his life. Walter Hughes had been one. He was the reason Sean made the money he did now and had the respect he had. Sean made a mental note to contact his old mentor to check in with him.

Sean knocked on her door and waited. Nothing. No sounds from her room. He frowned and raised his hand to knock again just as the door whooshed open. For the first few moments, his mind went blank. Every bit of brain activity dissolved. It wasn't a feeling he was accustomed to experiencing. For a former Army Special Forces and now well-known security expert, he normally could roll with any situation.

"Sean?"

He shook his head and brought his mind back to the present. Or at least somewhat. The woman was beautiful before, but she was stunning dressed as she was.

She'd pulled her natural curls up into some loose kind of bun in the back of her head, leaving a few wisps around her face. The dress she wore was made of some kind of soft, body hugging material

"Yeah, are you ready?"

How fucking lame could he get? She nodded, and stepped out of her room. He waited for her to walk by him, then followed her out of their suite.

"Make sure you call me Brett while we are around other people."

She slanted him a look as they walked side-by-side down the hallway. "What is it you Americans like to say? Oh, yes, this isn't my first rodeo."

Of course it wasn't. She was a seasoned agent and, if Lassiter trained her, there was a good chance she was almost as good as Sean. This was a complex and dangerous assignment. Letov was not a man to be fucked with, and while Lassiter liked to cut corners, he would never mess around with this situation. If he picked Jaime, she was up to the task.

Still, it didn't mean he wouldn't make sure she knew where they stood.

"Just don't fuck it up."

She said nothing as they stepped into the elevator, but she slanted him a look that would have killed a lesser man.

"And you might want to pretend that we are together."

She sighed. "Don't worry, love. I can handle faking it."

"Ah, so that's why you are in such a rotten mood."

She looked at him. "Why?"

"Well, if you are used to faking it…"

He let his insinuation sink it. He saw the moment it hit her. She frowned and stepped forward. Damn, she smelled good. Like *want to lick every inch of her flesh* good. She was definitely a treat he wanted to indulge in…again and again.

"I don't need you pulling shit on me tonight, S…Brett," she said, from behind clenched teeth. "If you can hold up your end, I can hold up mine."

He tried not to smile, but he couldn't really fight it.

"Don't you dare laugh," she said, but her tone had changed and her expression eased. She pulled back. "Wanker."

"Sorry."

She shook her head and wisps of her hair flowed with the movement. "No you aren't."

"Not really, but just remember that part of this job is fun."

She slanted a look from the side of her eye, but less threatening than the last. "Fun?"

He stepped closer, his body already humming with being so close to her. "We get to play with rich folks tonight. And, they will all be wondering about us, talking about us."

He took a chance and leaned down to brush his mouth over her shoulder. She shivered.

"I promise to make every woman in that place jealous."

Her tongue darted out over her lips and her pulse increased. He could see it in her neck, pounding away.

"Not the men?"

Oh, so she had heard about his tastes.

"Well, if you were interested in something like that, I could definitely accommodate, but at least for tonight, it would just be me and you."

Before she could answer, the doors slid open. He slipped his hand down to the small of her back and urged her out of the lift.

"You're very clever, aren't you?" she asked, her voice breathless.

"Oh, you have no idea." But Sean had all kinds of ideas to show her just how clever he was.

3

Jaime slipped her favorite tool into the keyhole. Her hands were shaking and her head was definitely not on the job. It was centered squarely on the man standing behind her.

"What's taking so long?" he asked.

His voice was just a breath of a whisper against her ear. He was so close he could nibble on her earlobe.

"Jaime?"

His lips brushed against her flesh.

She almost dropped her tools. *Dammit.* The man was doing it on purpose. He'd been bad all night and now that they were actually at the meat of their job, he was making it very difficult to concentrate. The rational part of her brain was telling her that it was her fault. He was just another sexy man. She'd dealt with enough of them in her lifetime. Her dealings with them had taught her to be wary. And that led her to the other thought—he was doing this on purpose.

She turned her head slightly so that their mouths were only centimeters apart. All she had to do was lean forward and their lips would be touching. Need soared. This close and she caught that exotic scent of him. Jaime knew Sean did not wear any cologne, so the intoxicating whiff she'd caught was all from the man. Her fingers itched to skim over that perfect skin.

But, she could not do it. And it showed her she needed to find a man and soon. Shagging someone like Sean was not a good idea. She used her best defense, her nasty personality.

"If you would kindly bugger off and take a step back, I can get it done."

Instead of doing as she ordered—as most men would when they heard the tone in her voice—his full, sensuous lips curved. "Can't handle a little pressure, Alexander?"

Dammit, she didn't want to be turned on by the question, and she definitely didn't want to be so attracted to the man. She wanted to be taken seriously in the business. Sleeping with any of her partners wasn't going to get her any respect, especially one like Sean. He had a reputation for being the best man to have your back, but he also had a reputation for being a bit of a slut—both ways. And *dammit*, his bisexuality made him even more exciting.

"I can handle it. I just don't like you breathing down my neck."

The knowing look in his eyes was enough to make her want to punch him. She would. Later. Now, she had to get them into the room. After a count back from ten, she slipped the tool in the slot again and got them in the room. Sean closed the door quietly behind them.

"Let's get these planted and get out of here."

She glanced at him. Even in the shadows, she saw that his teasing smile had dissolved into a determined scowl. She'd heard that he might like to play on the job, but when it came to work, he was all business.

"Are these even going to work in here?" she asked mostly to herself.

"First, Lassiter is a bastard, but he would not threaten our lives over something he thought we *might* be able to do. Secondly, yes." He glanced at the door. "Keep your ear to the door so I can get this one connected."

She nodded and did as he ordered. In less than five minutes, he had the bugs planted and they were ready to leave. It almost seemed too easy. She listened at the door, and heard footsteps. Holding up her hand, she stopped him and waited. Thank goodness the office was carpeted and the hallway was tiled. It was easy to hear the person walk away.

"Let's get the fuck out of here."

She nodded in agreement. She opened the door and peeked first left, then right. Once she was sure they were clear, Jamie stepped out into the hallway. It did not take that long to make it down the corridor. The elevator was in sight when they heard the voices. Russian.

Her heart hammered in her throat as she nodded, but he was already moving away from her.

"Fuck," Sean whispered. "This way."

Instead of turning in the opposite direction, he found a darkened corner and backed her into it. The voices drew closer and closer as he stepped in to her.

"Just follow my lead."

Before she could even think, Sean bent down in front of her and pushed up the skirt of her dress. Then, his large hands were on her thighs, pushing them apart. She didn't respond at first. She couldn't. Her brain shut down for a split second. The sick fear that had filled her moments ago changed into excitement. His breath feathered against her bare flesh and she shivered. Sean's hands were urging her legs apart, and she did as he silently ordered. Suddenly, his mouth was on her. His tongue slipped between her folds. She was already wet, dripping with arousal. The threat of danger always was a turn on for her and now, with this man's hands and tongue all over her, she couldn't stop from indulging.

She leaned her head back against the wall and moaned. Over

and over, he licked her as if she were a treat. The footsteps slowed, but they no longer mattered. A deep rich chuckle reached her, but she didn't give a bloody damn. All she cared about was this man and what he was making her feel. She was almost there, her orgasm just shimmering out of reach when he pulled away.

"What?" she said, barely able to form a coherent thought.

"Come on. We need to get out of here."

She blinked and looked around and realized they were alone. Her body was still humming, aching with a need for relief. Hell, she was pretty sure her thighs were still wet from his mouth, and he stood next to her acting as if nothing had happened.

With an aggravated sigh, Sean grabbed her hand and tugged her toward the elevator. They stepped in and he punched in the number to the ballroom floor. As the doors closed, she finally gathered her senses.

"You didn't have to do that."

Jaime kept her gaze on the doors. She couldn't look at him. She had been fully engaged in the act, but he had done it strictly for work.

"I did. Not only for safety either."

"That's as far as it will go."

"No, it isn't."

She felt his gaze flicker over her and, all of a sudden, she was in the corner again. He leaned down as he pressed his body against hers. It was impossible to ignore his erection. Jaime curled her fingers into her palm to keep from reaching out and stroking it.

He tugged on her earlobe, then said in a whisper, "We are going to finish it. I said that it wasn't *just* for safety. And even doubting me will get your ass smacked red."

"What if I say no?"

"You won't."

"But if I do?"

He shrugged. "Then, I walk away. But I promise you, I'll do my best to convince you."

Before she could respond, he moved away and the doors opened. Bloody hell, she had to get away from the man. He was making her like the sound of being spanked. She had always been open about her sexuality, but that had never been on the agenda. With him, though, it sounded splendid.

No. She could stop it. She could walk away and keep her sanity intact. As she stepped out of the lift, she glanced at him. The same knowing smile curved his lips and he winked at her.

Bloody hell, she was truly fucked.

4

As Sean followed Jaime into the hotel, his hands were practically shaking with need. That one little taste had his body raring to go. Of course, the lady in question was not really in the mood to discuss it. Since he had told her exactly what he was going to do to her, she had ignored him. He had wanted to flirt in the car on the way back, but he knew that even the slightest teasing would set him off. For a man who prided himself on his control, that was saying a lot.

They walked silently down the hall. There would be no debriefing tonight. Just in case something had gone wrong, Lassiter would not make contact. He had people at the hotel making sure they made it back unscathed. And they had, to an extent. Those few minutes with her had him ready to beg her for another chance.

He pulled out his key card and slipped it into the slot. Then, he held the door open and let her walk in. Damn, he could smell her. There was the scent of her perfume or soap or whatever. Roses. But then, the tantalizing aroma of her arousal still clung to her. And to him. Fuck, every time he swallowed he could taste her.

He let the door slam shut behind him and didn't move. He couldn't. Being this close to the bedrooms was a temptation. Well, fuck, being close to flat surfaces was enough to tempt him.

"When will we talk to Lassiter?" she asked.

She was looking out the window with her back to him. Sean frowned. She sounded as if she had gone back to her business-minded self. He did not like that one bit.

"Tomorrow or maybe Sunday. Unless there is an issue, we won't hear."

"Isn't that odd for a spy organization?"

He shook his head. "Legally, we are just contractors. The less contact we have, the easier it is for him to use us over and over."

Jaime nodded, but did not look at him. It was beyond irritating now.

"Jaime."

"What?"

The woman was almost as stubborn as he was. "Look at me."

At first, she did not move. She seemed to freeze for one long moment. Sean ground his teeth, and she took her time to do as he ordered.

"What?"

Damn, that sassy tone and her narrowed gaze should make him want to walk away. It didn't. She was a woman who presented all kinds of complications. He knew they would pair up well for work, and they had proven it tonight. Adding sex would only muddy the waters.

His raging hard-on didn't seem to give a fuck.

"Well?"

"Well, what?" he asked, trying to remember if she had asked him something. Jesus, he had no blood left in his brain. That could be the only explanation. He was amazed he was still able to form syllables.

"You said to look at you. I did. Now you're staring at me as if I've grown a second head."

"I…"

He couldn't come up with another word. He licked his lips and there was that taste of her again. Sweet, with a bit of sass. *Damn.*

"I know you play around on the job and that's fine. I'm just starting out; and while I don't mind working to gain respect, I don't want your kind of reputation."

"Why not?" he asked, then mentally kicked his ass. Seriously? He'd just asked her why she didn't want his kind of reputation. Where was the man who could seduce any woman or man out of their clothes?

"For a man, it's okay. In fact, it's expected. For women, it's different."

That stopped him. "That's sexist."

She shrugged. "I didn't say I agreed with it. It actually sucks for someone like me. I just said that is the way it is."

"Well, it's a cop out on your part. How is anyone going to find out?"

One perfectly sculpted eyebrow rose. "Don't you kiss and tell?"

"No."

She rolled her eyes. "Sean, everyone knows about your conquests."

"Not because of me. I don't run around screaming about how many women or men I have slept with. It's nobody's fucking business."

"It isn't the way to start off my contracting career."

She was saying that, but there was something beneath the tone. Something that told him that she did want more. He walked to her, slowly.

"How about we do this? Why not just tonight? No one has to know."

At first, she did not respond. Then, she shook her head. "Everyone will know."

"How?" he asked, as he took her hand. He pulled her closer. "I'm not going to tell them."

She sighed. "They'll know."

"How? No recording devices, and you know Lassiter won't say anything."

He urged her closer so their bodies touched. God, she felt good. All those smooth curves pressed against him.

"Sean." Her voice shook.

"Jaime."

Her lips twitched. "This can't go anywhere."

He bent his head and nipped at the gorgeous neck. "I have to disagree. It can go to all kinds of interesting places."

She held her spine straight until he slid his tongue from her collarbone up to her jaw. She shivered, and he felt her surrender right there and then.

"Do you play?"

She turned to face him. "Play?"

"Bondage."

She shook her head.

"Tell you what. We'll try some fun things tonight. Just a little fun…nothing hard-core. You tell me if you don't like it."

She pulled her bottom lip between her teeth and nodded. That little show of vulnerability warned him to be cautious. Jaime was a woman who would not like to be seen as having any vulnerability. So, he needed to take it slow. Or, as slowly as he would be able to manage.

He lowered his head as he turned her toward him. He brushed his mouth over hers and then dove inside. Need built, as his heart pounded against his chest.

By the time he pulled back, they were both breathing heavily. He had been honest. He had wanted to take this slowly. Something was telling him it was important, and he always listened to his instincts.

He took her hand and led her into his bedroom. He left her

standing as he took his seat in the chair. He said nothing for a long moment. Jaime was a woman of action, and it would definitely drive her a little crazy having to stand there.

"What now?" she asked.

He wanted to smile, but he didn't. He didn't want her to know he was amused. He wanted to keep her off-center.

"Strip."

5

For one really long moment, Jaime's brain short-circuited. It wasn't something she had ever done for a man before—not even for money. She'd always said she could hold her head high because she had not stripped or sold her body. There were things she had done in the past that would make most good women balk, but that stepped over a line. Add to that, she had never been a woman who liked to be told what to do.

But with this man it was different.

Mentally, she shook her head. No, it wasn't. It was the adrenaline from the night's work. Of course, his very talented mouth and tongue had a lot to do with it.

"I'm waiting, Jaime."

His voice wasn't as playful as before. There was a touch of the command she had heard earlier when they were on the job. She raised her gaze to his and was greeted with a stony stare. This was a different man than the one who had flirted. This one liked control—thrived on it. And in that split instant, she knew he would walk away if she didn't do as he ordered. Worse, she wanted to please him. Oddly, there was a part of her that yearned to make him happy. It was as if there was some kind of connection with him.

There was something really wrong with her if a man she had only known for hours had her doing a strip tease.

"If you've changed your mind, that's fine."

She heard it in his voice. He was warning her if she didn't, she would not be rewarded.

And what the hell was the reward?

Him.

She had been a woman who had survived thanks to a quick-thinking mind. She had refused entanglements, and Sean was one big entanglement. But she wanted this. She wanted to give in for this one night and complete what they had started.

She bent over to rid herself of her shoes, but he stopped her. "No, leave those on. And the hair—I like it that way."

Yes, he was in command, but there was a hint of heat in his voice. He was not as unaffected as he was pretending to be. She glanced down and had to fight the smile. Definitely not in complete control, if indicated by his erection.

"Time's wasting. You don't get to see my cock until I see those breasts and your tasty pussy."

She shivered. The naughty promise sent little sparks of electricity dancing over her nerve endings.

She lifted her hands to unzip her dress. She had nothing on beneath it. The anticipation of his reaction to that increased her arousal. Her sex was already dripping wet.

With slow movements, she slipped the straps off her shoulders then let her dress fall to the ground.

"All bare…I like that in a woman. Knowing that you're walking around with nothing but flesh beneath your clothes is very arousing. I like to know that I can take a lover to a corner, bend her over and fuck her right there."

"Or him."

He smiled and nodded. "Definitely."

He said nothing else for a few moments. The balls of her feet actually tingled. The need to move almost overwhelmed her. Then he lifted his hand and motioned. She hesitated and then did as he ordered.

"Turn around."

She did and was rewarded. The palm of his hand connected with the full part of her ass; afterwards, rubbing over the tender flesh. In the next moment, she felt his breath feather over her skin right before his mouth touched her. Over and over, he smoothed his hands over her rear end as he kissed and nipped at the same time. It was simple and very arousing. He slipped his hands up to her waist and urged her around to face him.

He leaned forward and took one nipple into his mouth as he slid a hand down to her sex. After thrusting a finger into her, he hummed against her nipple. The action vibrated over her flesh and shot straight to her pussy.

He pulled back and smiled up at her, his eyes barely opened. "Oh, someone is hurting, aren't ya, baby?"

She hated that term, but for some reason, when he called her baby, she liked it. She said nothing but nodded.

He pulled his finger out of her. "On your knees, kitten. I think I deserve a little bit of payback for earlier."

She did and waited.

"Unzip my pants."

She did and his erection sprang forward. He was so damn big. A little bit of precum wet the head.

"In your mouth."

She didn't even hesitate. She leaned forward and he stopped her.

"Hands behind your back."

Need lanced through her as she did as he ordered once again. She took him in her mouth and started to suck. It took a lot of work to keep herself steady, moving over his hard cock. Soon, though, his fingers slipped into her hair dislodging some of her pins. She paid no attention. He moaned as he molded his hands to the back of her head. Jaime hummed and he groaned loud, but he did not come. Instead, he pulled her back as he reached toward the table beside the chair. After ripping open the condom wrapper, he rolled it on, then he grabbed her, tugging her onto his lap.

She rocked her hips, pulling another groan from him. "Put me inside of you."

Jaime cocked her head and studied him. "So, I'm allowed to use my hands again?"

He chuckled. "Yes."

It was all she needed. Taking his cock in one hand, she slid down on him. Slowly, she moved, up and down, teasing them both with the possibilities. He pulled her close and took a nipple in his mouth once again, sucking, nipping, licking. Then, he urged her head closer so that he could kiss her.

Still, she kept the pace slow and easy. With a growl, he stood up, and walked to the bed. Once there, he took her hips into his hands, rose to his knees, and started to thrust in and out of her. Before she was prepared for it, her orgasm slammed through her. It hit so bloody fast, she screamed at the force of the sensation. But, he was not done. Over and over, he pushed her, threw her over that edge. By the time he followed her, she was worn out, not able to think straight. He collapsed a moment later on top of her.

She wrapped her arms around him. "You do know how to end a job right, Kaheaku."

He chuckled and turned his head so he could nibble on her chin.

"Give me a few moments and I'll really show you a good end."

"Is that a fact?"

He raised himself off the bed and looked at her. "Yeah, unless once was enough for you."

"Well, it wasn't exactly once."

His mouth twitched. He leaned down to brush his mouth over hers. "I promise you, once was definitely not enough."

She said nothing, but smiled. As he laid his head back down and snuggled closer to her, she realized that he was right. Jaime also realized she was probably completely over her head with him.

But if growing up on the street had taught her one thing, it was to live in the moment. Right now, this man was her moment, and she was definitely going to enjoy him.

∽

The next morning, Sean slipped back into bed. He pulled Jaime against him.

"Where were you?"

"Phone. We have a briefing at three tomorrow."

"Hmm," she said, her voice drowsy with contentment. He loved the way she looked in the morning. The first rays of the sun were peeking through the curtains, leaving the room in a soft glow. She looked like a painting.

"What?" she asked. He looked down at her face, but her eyes were still closed.

"Lassiter wanted to know if we wanted to work another job together."

She said nothing. He needed to do something, so he traced his finger over her bare shoulder. Her flesh was so silky, as if she bathed in lotion.

"What are your thoughts?" she asked in a neutral voice. When he glanced down at her face, he saw a flash of vulnerability there. It touched his heart.

"I said I would have to talk it over with you first. I had a feeling it is why we were paired up. Lassiter knows what kind of partner I like."

"Oh, does he?"

He chuckled. "Not in bed. Definitely a straight shooter there. No, I like someone who is quick on his or her feet and doesn't mind improvising. I think even with that little mishap last night, we both handled it well."

She smiled. "I did like it."

"So, how about it. Ever been to Monte Carlo?"

She blinked. "No. I've never left England."

"Well, then, Ms. Alexander, I think we have the beginnings of a great partnership."

She didn't respond with a smile as he had hoped. She sighed. "What about this?"

He studied her for a long moment. "Not a requirement, but I definitely like it as a benefit."

She nodded and cuddled closer.

"Good, but now we have to talk about other things."

"What kind of things?" she asked before licking his nipple. Damn, the woman was going to be the death of him.

He slipped out of bed and tugged her to the edge, then up into his arms. He carried her to the bathroom.

"Why don't we talk about those things in the shower?"

She laughed. "Sounds good, *partner*."

A very good start in his opinion, but he had a few ideas on just how to validate her faith in him—and they had a whole day for him to do it.

II

PRELUDE TO A REVENGE, PART TWO

1

Sean studied the overhead screen and fought the need to curse. This was going to be a shit job. Sure, it was going to bring in some much-needed capital, but he didn't know if it was going to be worth it. Now that he knew the risks, he was starting to have second thoughts—especially with a new partner.

He glanced at Randy Young. When Lassiter had first told him whom he was working with, Sean wasn't all that thrilled. The newest member of Lassiter's motley band of contractors wasn't Sean's first pick, but he would do for this kind of job. As a former SEAL, Young had the experience. Young must have felt his study and gave Sean an understanding nod. He thought the job sucked too.

It was hard to get a handle on the newest member of Lassiter's team. He was a fucking god built of muscles and California good looks, hot enough to make Sean drool. But there was a brain in there too. Knowing he swung both ways like Sean made him almost irresistible. Young had been working his way through just about all of the operatives, with the exception of Sean.

The man was long and lean, just about as tall as Sean, with laughing blue eyes. From the smooth, tanned flesh, he had been spending a lot of time on the California beaches, but for some reason, Sean was sure he was tan from the tips of his toes to the top of his head.

Fuck, he didn't need to become preoccupied with another operative. He needed to focus on the job at hand, no matter how much of a FUBAR it was.

"I don't like the idea," Sean said. "We have to go in blind?"

Lassiter nodded. "Yeah, and I know it sucks."

"It's beyond sucking," Randy said, his voice deadly calm and his usually jovial mood absent. "It could end up with both of us dead."

Lassiter shook his head. "You military folk always look at everything in worst-case scenario."

Lassiter had never been in the military. MI-6 was his only training and that's why he had no problems cutting corners or taking chances—as long as other people were at risk. Sean was former Army and with Randy being a former SEAL, they both knew too well what could go wrong.

"It's one way to make sure we arrive alive," Sean said.

He didn't mind taking chances, but he really did not like the idea of a suicide mission. This definitely had those markings and not for anything noble. Saving a life, that would have been worth it, but for money—no matter how much—he wasn't sure this was worth it.

"I wouldn't send you if I thought there was a chance you'd be attacked," his boss said, his voice as cool as it had been over the last year. Sean had started working for him when he and Jaime had broken it off. Well, more like she had broken it off, and Sean had left MI-6 for a fresh start. Lassiter apparently blamed Sean, even though he was the one who had wanted more. At least Lassiter had hired him outright.

"What is actually the reason we are going?" Young asked. His new partner was definitely not sold on the mission.

"Missionaries."

A LITTLE HARMLESS REVENGE

Sean paused. "We're going after missionaries?"

"They need transportation out. I had one of their friends contact me. He is the one promising the money."

"Who is after missionaries?" Young asked.

"They aren't your average missionaries. Rich do-gooders who have caught the attention of an Islamic terrorist group. MILF."

"MILF?" Sean asked.

"The Moro Islamic Liberation Front."

"And I take it they want the young do-gooders' money," Young said.

Sean nodded. Kidnappings were on the rise in Southeast Asia. Unfortunately, even if the kidnappers were paid on time, the chances their prey was still alive was slim to none. Still, most people would take that chance if it meant saving a loved one.

"But, no contact?" Young asked.

"Sean knows the area."

Young glanced at him. It was the first time since they had been sitting side-by-side in front of Lassiter's desk that he had. The full attention of those deep blues short-circuited his brain for a few seconds.

"Do you think it's worth it?"

Sean shrugged then looked at Lassiter. "You said they are in hiding? No one has found them?"

Lassiter nodded. "Being rich does have its benefits, and they have paid people well to hide them."

Young read over the report and nodded. "Yeah. Doesn't mean I like it. The area we are going into is overwhelmed with terrorist groups. They use it as a training area. Hell, so did we."

"Legally?" Sean asked.

Young's lips twitched. "No comment."

"The other problem is the coverage in the area. I know this area. Cell sucks and even satellite reception has issues. We get stuck, there might be no way to get out."

Apparently, Lassiter had had enough. "I'm pretty sure I can

find someone else to handle it for the money, but, you two are my best bets."

Sean glanced at Young and nodded again. "I can handle the money *and* the situation."

Young's eyes twinkled as his lips curved. "Most definitely."

Sean just hoped once they got to where they were going, they got out free and fast.

2

"Something's fucked," Randy Young said, his tone as dark as his scowl.

They'd arrived just moments before, both of them relieved on how easy it had been. Then, they had stepped inside. There was something very, very wrong. Sean could feel it in his bones.

Sean glanced at Young, then around the abandoned hut. He had to agree with the former SEAL. There was something really fucking wrong with the situation.

Dust covered the furnishings, and there were definitely signs of decay. The small wooden table looked like termites or something had been eating on it. Hell, the covers on the small cot were moving. The stench of rotting vegetation permeated the air. He really didn't want to know what was living under there. The absence of any humans—along with any kind of food told him one thing.

"No one has been here in months," he said. He rolled his shoulders as a dribble of sweat slid down his spine. Fuck, it was hot.

Young nodded. "So, did Lassiter set us up, or did someone set up Lassiter and we get caught up in it?"

"That's a very good question."

His gut clenched. Damn, he didn't want to think badly of his old friend, but things weren't adding up. Lassiter had never had a clusterfuck like this in the years Sean had been working for him. He'd trusted the man with his life more than once, but now he was having doubts.

Maybe Lassiter was more pissed about his breakup with Jaime than Sean had thought. Sean knew Lassiter had trained her, had guided her through her career, and he had taken it personally when Sean and Jaime split up. Still, Sean didn't think Lassiter would set him up to be killed for it.

Sean glanced around again. There weren't even any signs the missionaries had been there. It was a dead end. No one had been there for at least a month, probably more. Just as both he and Young had worried, there was something off about the mission.

"You've worked for him for awhile. Do you think he'd set us up like this?"

Sean glanced at Young. He was fucking smart, and it wasn't as if Sean hadn't just had the same thought.

"I haven't given him reason to. Have you?"

A smile that had nothing to do with humor curled Young's lips. Damn, it made him even more fuckable. Sean always liked his humor with a dark and sadistic edge, and especially appreciated it in his lovers.

Fuck. He needed to get his mind off *that* topic. They needed to formulate a plan that had to deal with getting the fuck out of there.

"So, you're relationship with Lassiter is contingent on you not giving him a reason to kill you?"

He smiled. "That's pretty much true in all of my relationships."

Young chuckled at that. "Same here. What the fuck do you think it means?"

"I think he has bad info, or someone is setting us up."

"Ya think?"

"Who have *you* pissed off lately?" Sean asked.

"My parents, my old commanding officer. Oh, and some woman on the 405 last week, but I don't think I have pissed off anyone enough for this."

"Then you aren't living your life right."

They shared another smile, then they both went back to inspecting the room. Instinct and experience told him with the small click he'd heard; they had tripped some kind of alarm. Thank Jesus it was only an alarm and not a tripwire to a bomb. His heartbeat jumped up a few thousand beats as he glanced at his companion. Young raised one eyebrow. The former SEAL had heard it too.

"Let's get the fuck out of here," he said, his voice eerily calm.

Sean nodded and followed him out of the hut they had found. They had no idea how long it would be before someone showed up, and there was no use sticking around to find out. He followed Randy out of the hut and down the path they had taken. He held up his fist, indicating to hold position. Sean did as told. He had no problem taking orders from the SEAL. They both had about the same amount of experience, and there was something about a man who knew how to give as good as he got—in more ways than one.

Thwap, thwap, thwap…footsteps hurried toward them. Again, instinct saved both of them. From the sound of it, they had too many people to go up against. There were at least ten of them heading in their direction. While Sean didn't mind a good fight, he didn't believe in suicide missions.

Young motioned with his head and Sean followed. He was the better of the two at tracking and finding his way out of a shit situation. This was definitely a shit situation. They had gone in under the cover of night, no support. It had been a bad situation all around, but it had paid good money. Now, he was starting to understand just why.

Shots rang out behind them, but neither of them stopped to answer the attack. They knew they were outnumbered. As their pursuers continued to shoot, Young and Sean put some space between them. When Young led them out to a road, Sean almost ran into the back of him.

"Hey," Young said.

"Well, I didn't know you were going to come to a stop like that."

Then, Sean looked around. "I know this area."

Young glanced at him. "You do?"

He heard the skepticism and shook his head. He noticed a cargo truck sitting on the side of the road. "We can't stand here and discuss it. We need to get the fuck out of here, and I know a place we can stay."

This time he took the lead, going across the road then back into the jungle. He knew if they got to the next road over, they were home free. They could definitely get a ride into Bulusan there and get the fuck off the island.

Then, another shot rang out from behind them. It flew past Sean and hit the tree by his head. A piece of bark from the trunk flew off and hit him in the forehead.

"Motherfuck."

It wasn't that big, but the sharp edge of it had connected with his head. His first instinct was to move forward, but he heard Young stumble. When Sean turned around, Young staggered to his feet. His partner looked down at his upper arm.

"Fucking hell."

A basic flesh wound, but Sean knew it probably stung like a bitch.

"Come on."

"Go, keep going. There's only one."

Sean shook his head and hurried back to him. "You go, I'll watch your back."

Young agreed and went on his way. Sean stood still watching

the forest, then he saw the flash of movement. He raised his rifle and waited. Movement again, and Sean took a shot. There was a yell, then cursing in a language he didn't know, but he was pretty sure it was Eastern European of some sort.

"Kaheaku, what the fuck?"

"Go," he said turning back to Young. "I know a place up here we can stay, no questions, and we can dress that wound."

"Who did you just shoot?"

"I have a feeling it was supposed to be their lookout."

Young opened his mouth, but Sean wasn't in the mood for it. "Just fucking go. I don't want to wait for the others to catch up."

Young did as Sean had ordered, and he followed his partner as he tried to figure out just what the hell had happened, and just how the hell they would get themselves out of the mess.

3

Randy had been in some horrible situations before this. There was the time he'd been pinned down outside of Kandahar, and they had lost three of the team members. He'd lost another one of his former SEAL team members to suicide when he couldn't cope with the memories. None of that could compare to the clusterfuck this assignment had brought about.

"Up here," Kaheaku said. He glanced at his partner and nodded. Randy's pain was escalating with each step he took. Worse, he kept thinking about infection. He just wanted to get it cleaned out and dressed. Running around the jungle was probably not a good idea with an open wound.

They stepped into a clearing. There was a building there, which apparently operated as some sort of hotel. He glanced at Kaheaku, who shrugged.

"Not the greatest accommodations, but I figured a former SEAL could handle it."

Randy nodded and followed him up. There was very little activity around it, but it was pretty evident he was one of the very few Caucasians in the area. Add in that most of the men refused to make eye contact. Uneasiness slipped down his spine.

"Aren't you worried we'll get noticed?"

Sean shook his head. "No. Most of these people don't want anyone to know what they're doing. Not here anyway."

Randy studied the group again. Some were dressed in clothes similar to what he and Kaheaku wore. Cargo pants, t-shirts, boots. But, there were men in business suits, and almost everyone there was male. And the men were the only ones in couples. It hit him that this was probably secluded for a reason.

He glanced at his companion again. "Is there a reason you know about this place?"

His lips twitched before they curved into a cocky smile. "Other than the fact that I needed a place to stay after my car went out on me last year, no. I don't hide my sexual preferences."

Fuck, the man was sexy. Randy had noticed him from the first moment he'd started working for Lassiter. It was hard not to. Tall, muscled, green eyes—right up Randy's alley. Knowing Kaheaku was bisexual added to the attraction, but worse, he was fucking sarcastic. It made him almost impossible not to fantasize about.

He'd taken time to fashion a bandage out of a bandana, but the blood was starting to seep through. And he needed to give the wound a good cleaning.

Sean apparently read his mind.

"Let's get a room and get you set. Then we can figure out what to do."

He nodded and followed Sean up the front steps. A small Filipino man stood behind a stained desk.

"Need a room," Sean said.

Randy noticed he did not ask, just ordered. He liked that in a man…to a point. And in the situation, it was definitely nice. Randy was accustomed to taking charge, and he was good at it. But, his arm ached and he was starting to feel a little lightheaded. Having someone take over the little things at the moment made life a little easier.

The man behind the counter said nothing back to Sean. Apparently they knew each other well enough. He grabbed a key and flung it on the desk. Sean tossed out a few bills, grabbed the key.

"Let's go," he said, without turning around.

Randy wasn't that great at taking orders. It was one of the reasons he had left the Navy. He'd loved his job, but he did better working with a two-person team. Share the work. He definitely didn't like working for jackasses like his last commanding officer. But, right now, it was just best to go along.

He followed Kaheaku up two sets of stairs. Sweat trickled down his back and his arm throbbed. The thing hurt like a motherfucker. If Kaheaku hadn't shot the bastard, Randy would have been tempted to hunt the bastard down and beat the shit out of him.

By the time they reached the room, Randy could barely catch his breath. It was embarrassing to admit, even to himself.

Kaheaku unlocked the door and stepped inside. They both surveyed the room. It wasn't big. Hell, there wasn't a lot of space in the room.

"We need to get that cut cleaned and dressed."

Randy looked around the room again, then walked to the bathroom. "I might catch something else in here."

Kaheaku shook his head as he took off his pack. "I got supplies, as I am sure you do as well."

He did. "I can take care of it."

Kaheaku let one brow rise but said nothing. Of course he didn't. He wasn't truly the leader of the partnership, but in a way he was. He'd known Lassiter longer than Randy had and he was uninjured.

"Okay."

He stripped off his shirt and winced as a fission of pain shot down his arm.

"Fuck," he said from behind gritted teeth. Shit, he didn't want to look weak now. It was stupid, but it was like he was trying to impress Kaheaku. They both crowded into the bathroom.

"Ah, really just a flesh wound."

He nodded. Kaheaku opened a bottle of antiseptic and poured it on Randy's wound.

"Mother fuck."

Kaheaku chuckled. "Yeah, I bet that hurts. I think I'm gonna have to sew it up. Butterfly sutures are not going to work."

"And the day just keeps getting better," Randy said as he watched Kaheaku pull out a needle and thread. "Listen, I know you're former Special Forces, but do you know what you're doing with that thing?"

A small smile curved his lips. "Yeah. I grew up on a ranch on the Big Island, so I know all about taking care of injuries."

"Hawaii?"

He nodded. Randy should have known it from the cadence in Kaheaku's voice, not to mention the last name.

"And, up in cattle country, it could be a long drive to the hospital. You learn how to fix things like this."

He threaded the needle as if trained and Randy swallowed. He had hunted the Taliban, faced down more than one insurgent in Iraq, but fucking needles freaked him the fuck out.

"Don't worry. I'll be gentle."

The double entendre surprised a laugh out of him.

"I just have this thing with needles."

"Yeah. My mom did too. She would freak out if there was even mention of a needle."

"Was?"

"She died a few years ago."

And it was a soft spot for the big Hawaiian. He heard it in Kaheaku's voice that he still missed his mother. Dammit, it only made him even more attractive.

Over the next few minutes, they didn't speak. Kaheaku worked the needle in and out of his skin as Randy did his best not to vomit or, worse, pass out. When Kaheaku finally finished, Randy released a breath he did not know he had been holding.

"Take the bed and catch a few minutes. I'll survey the perimeter."

He opened his mouth, but Sean shook his head. "You need to rest up and then you can take over. I want to make sure you don't get an infection. I am not about to carry your ass out of here."

He smiled and watched as Kaheaku packed away the medical supplies.

"I'll hunt up some drinking water so you can take a couple of ibuprofen."

He nodded and didn't argue. Kaheaku left him alone. He sat down on the bed and looked around. Damn, he was getting old if one little flesh wound had him down for the count.

There was one thing that was for sure, once he got a hold of Royce Lassiter, he was going to beat the shit out of the man.

~

THREE HOURS LATER, SEAN KEPT WATCH BY THE WINDOW. NIGHT had fallen quickly and though it seemed their tail had disappeared, something was wrong. There was something really off about this assignment from the start, and it was going downhill fast.

Young shifted on the mattress, drawing Sean's attention. He walked over and looked down at his partner. He had checked under the bandage in the last hour, and there was no redness around the wound yet. That had eased some of his worries. Now, though, Young didn't look so hot. Sweat beaded his brow and his skin was flush. Fever had set in, but Sean didn't think it had to do with the wound. Dammit. Could anything else go wrong?

This assignment was definitely fucked.

4

For a full two days, Sean was stuck at the hotel. Randy's fever kept him in bed for twenty-four hours. He could have left him, and Randy had tried to get him to go, but it was too dangerous. Randy would be left with no way of defending himself. When the fever finally broke, he could barely get the energy to move. It took another twenty-four hours before Sean was able to leave so he could contact Lassiter.

"I should be back within a few hours. Hopefully, I can get a hold of Lassiter without too much trouble."

Randy nodded. "Tell him I'm not all that thrilled working for him."

"Will do."

But he hesitated.

"Go. I can deal with the situation."

He did as Randy ordered and started off to the nearest town. He needed to get somewhere with good cell reception. Sean knew he had limited time before he was recognized, and he also had limited time he could leave Randy. He had to admit; it hadn't been as uncomfortable as he thought it would be. Caring for someone he wasn't really familiar with should have been awkward, but it wasn't. They seemed to have a connection. Most of it probably had to do with the situation. Desperate times and close quarters helped diminish any normal barriers. Sean figured they would sort out what it meant between them later.

He didn't have to go into Bulusan, but he knew he needed to get as close as possible. And they needed to get the fuck away from there. They were very close to an active volcano and, going by the rest of the mission, Sean didn't want to take any chances.

As soon as the satellite phone picked up a signal, he dialed Lassiter. They weren't supposed to have support, but he knew his boss would want to hear from them. Lassiter picked up on the first ring.

"Where the fuck are you?" Lassiter growled into the phone.

"Well, hello to you too."

"Sean, don't fuck with me. We've had our hands full trying to find you. Is Young there?"

"No. He's back in the room."

"Injuries?"

"Young, but just a flesh wound. You want to tell me what the hell is going on?"

Lassiter sighed. "You were hit the same time Jaime was."

Even after the year apart, his heart lodged somewhere in his throat. He didn't think he would ever get over her. "Is she okay?"

"Yeah." He sighed, sounding weary now. "She's doing fine now."

Sean wanted to ask more, but he knew Lassiter well enough to know that he wouldn't tell Sean any more.

"So, you're saying this was planned?"

"Yes, and it has to do with something you two must have worked on, but I have yet to figure out what it is. I have a transport I can set up on my command. How soon can the two of you get to Bulusan?"

"Slow down. Can't travel for another day or two."

"I thought you said Young was okay."

"He is, but he had some kind of flu. It knocked him down. It will take at least another twenty-four hours. Also, he doesn't trust you much right now."

"Damn, and we need him. I'll make sure to make it up to both of you. Be there on Thursday, midnight, your time. Chuck is going to pick you up."

He knew the man well, and Lassiter knew that. Especially since they didn't know who to trust at the moment.

"Gotcha. So, is Jaime going to be okay?"

"She's fine. We should be back in the states by the time you two get back. Maybe we can put our heads together and figure something out."

"Got it. See you in a few days."

He turned off the phone and started on his way back. It wasn't going to be an easy trip. While Randy had finally gotten some energy, a trek through the rainforest over mountainous areas was going to be hard. They could make it to Bulusan by Wednesday no problem. It gave them three days.

It took him less time to make it back, or at least it seemed like it did. He still tried his best to muddy up his trail just in case anyone was following him. They didn't need any more problems on this mission.

When he arrived back at the room, Randy was sitting on the bed, ready to go. His pack was beside him, and he was dressed.

"Do we have a transport?"

Sean nodded.

"Let's go."

"Don't you think you should take a little more time?"

The look Randy gave him told him exactly where he thought Sean could stick that idea.

"No. I have a bad feeling, and those usually pan out. We need to get out of here as fast as possible."

"We have until Thursday at midnight."

"Someone you trust is going to pick us up?"

Sean nodded. "I've worked with Chuck. Former SEAL like yourself, but he lost a leg, so he's been doing transports."

"Good. Let's go. It seems there is a break in the weather, but I heard a couple of the guys talking, and they said they expect a bitch of a storm in about thirty-six hours. We have got to get there before the rain hits."

"Fuck, this job has been shitty from the first moment we landed. I have to tell you something." Randy stopped moving and looked at him. "This might have been a retaliatory hit for something I did with my old partner. She got hit around the same time we did."

Randy sighed. "Well, shit. Is she okay?"

"Yeah. Lassiter is with her wherever she is."

"Yeah. Let's get to Bulusan. Last time I was there, I stayed at a nice little resort. They don't ask questions, especially for the extra cash.

"I think we should lay low."

Randy shrugged. "The bastards after us are probably long gone. But, if they aren't, they won't be looking for us at the resort. Plus, we can just hang out in the room."

He wanted to say no, and his training told him he should, but instead, he studied Randy. He was a bit pale, and Sean knew he had also dropped a few pounds.

"Listen, I want to make sure that you don't catch whatever I have. If we're stuck out in the jungle hiding and you get sick, we'll miss the transport. At least this way we have a better chance of making it."

He couldn't really argue with that and, at the moment, he wanted to just sleep for days. This would give them the option.

"Let's go."

Randy smiled. "Great. I'm sure we can come up with something to do with all that time."

5

Randy settled back on the clean bed and sighed. Sean had let him take the shower first, and he was glad of it. It had taken them about a day to get to the resort, and the only room left had a king bed and was way in the back away from most of the hustle and bustle. Perfect for them…in more ways than one.

The trip had not been easy, and if Sean hadn't been so handy with hotwiring a car, they would still be making their way there.

Randy studied the door to the bathroom. The water was still running, and he could just imagine it sliding over all that gorgeous tanned skin. There was no doubt about it; Sean Kaheaku was a Hawaiian god. He had gotten a good look at him over the last few days, and the more and more Randy saw, the more he wanted. He knew enough about the man to know that Sean swung both ways, and since Randy did too, he figured it wouldn't be a problem. He'd also done a damn good job taking care of him. Not a lot of guys were good in that situation, but Sean had stepped up to the plate.

The water turned off. Randy picked up a mango and started munching on it. He needed something to occupy his time while he came up with a plan. He really didn't want to rock the boat. Things seemed to click for them from the moment they started the mission. If he came on to Sean, and he wasn't interested, that was okay with Randy. But, they had two more days left in the room, and he wasn't in the mood to deal with the tension after that. Especially since there was no way for him to work through his frustration.

The door opened and all of his second thoughts faded away. Sean was standing in the doorway, a towel around his waist and his hair brushed back from his face. A little bit of scruff covered his jaw. Damn, the man was fucking sexy.

"What?" Sean said. Randy heard the deepening in his partner's voice.

He tossed the rest of his mango in the nearby trash and rose from the bed. Without breaking his stride, he walked to Sean, then stopped, leaving less than an inch between them. They were about the same height, so their mouths were level. He cupped Sean's face with both hands, rubbing his thumbs over his whiskers. He smelled of the soap they had both used and for some reason, Randy found that so damned erotic.

"This is probably a mistake," Randy said.

Sean's mouth curved. "Yeah."

"Fuck it."

Randy slammed his mouth against Sean's, thrusting his tongue inside. Instantly, arousal spiked, his cock hardening almost immediately. The need had been simmering there since the moment he had been paired up with Sean. Now, it was time to enjoy it.

He pulled back, and yanked the towel free from Sean's waist. Fuck, he was just as aroused as Randy, his cock curving up against his belly. He reached down, wrapped his hand around it, and gave it a long stroke. He continued as he looked up at Sean's face.

His eyes slid closed, as he bent his head back against the wall.

"Fuck."

"Yeah, sounds about right," Randy said. He squeezed Sean's cock and it jerked in his hand. "And you like it a little rough."

Sean said nothing as Randy continued to stroke him. He knew he was close, but Randy wanted a taste. He dropped to his knees in front of Sean and took him in his mouth. The salty sweet flavor of his cum hit him first, his cock responding as it slid over his taste buds. Randy slipped his hand down to his sac and squeezed. Sean shuddered as he slid his fingers through Randy's hair. He wanted to push the control freak over the edge, so Randy slipped his hands around to his ass, pulling his cheeks apart. As he slipped his finger between, Sean shouted and thrust deep into his Randy's mouth.

Moments later, he fell back against the wall as Randy gave his cock one last lick.

He stood up and kissed him. His own body was begging for release. When he pulled back from the kiss, he waited for Sean to open his eyes. "Ready for round two?"

Sean nodded. "I definitely want a taste."

"Yeah, I want that talented mouth on me, but not this time."

He pulled away from Sean and tugged him over to the bed. They both worked to get his pants undone and off his body. When they were both standing naked, Sean stepped closer to press his body against Randy's. Even though he had just had a release, his cock was hardening. It touched against Randy's shaft, and he almost came right there and then. He couldn't remember needing a release so badly.

Sean moved closer, but instead of kissing him on the lips, he leaned down and set his mouth against his neck. He licked Randy's pulse point.

"Fuck."

Sean chuckled and nipped at his jaw. "Such impatience. I'd think a SEAL would have better control."

When Sean met his gaze, he saw the heat he was feeling reflected back.

"And, you think you want to teach me how to control myself?"

"Is that an invitation?"

He hesitated. He was used to being the aggressor, so he was in unfamiliar territory.

"I promise to be gentle," Sean said, his voice filled with humor.

"Fuck that."

Sean's smile turned into a grin. In that moment, Randy knew he was in trouble. He barely knew the man, and making him happy caused Randy more joy than he wanted to admit. He wanted to see that smile all the time.

Sean gave him a long, wet kiss, then he turned to grab his pack. He pulled out a condom.

He blinked. "Damn, you *do* always come prepared."

He didn't put the condom on though. Instead, he dropped to a squat and took Randy's cock into his mouth.

"Ah, fuck," he said.

Sean definitely had a talented mouth, just as he had known he would. Sean pushed him to the edge several times, his tongue gliding over Randy's rigid flesh. He knew just how to work his shaft over, teasing him enough to drive him crazy, but held back. Each time Randy thought he was going to come, Sean pulled back. The last time, he grabbed Randy's cock and held it up to give him access to his sac. One long lick over his sac had Randy shaking.

"Fuck me."

Sean rose to his feet. "Gladly."

It wasn't so much of an invitation, but he definitely didn't give a fuck. He was in the mood to have a cock up his ass, anything to get Sean to let him come.

He slipped the condom on, as Randy got up on all fours on

the bed. Sean joined him with a tube of lube he hadn't seen before.

"Yeah, I always come prepared, but not *that* prepared. I picked it up when I bought the food."

Randy turned around as Sean slipped a finger into his ass. He worked his second finger in, then he removed his fingers and pulled Randy's ass cheeks apart and started to enter him. Slowly, almost as if he wanted to enjoy every inch, he sunk into Randy. He was fucking big, but he finally got to the small ring of muscles and pushed through. It had been a while since he had bottomed, and it left him a little tense. If Sean noticed, he said nothing. Slowly, he worked himself in and out of Randy's ass, taking it slowly and not pushing too hard. Randy pushed back against him, needing it harder, wanting a bit of pain, but that earned him a slap on the ass.

"Don't rush me."

He kept the rhythm slow and easy, allowing their need to build steadily. But, soon, even Sean seemed to want to speed things up. Then, he was thrusting in and out of Randy's ass, his strokes measured and deep. His fingers dug into his cheeks and Randy welcomed the pain. He needed something to keep him from coming. He wanted to let the pleasure stretch. Fuck, he never wanted it to end.

Soon, though, Sean reached around and tugged on Randy's cock. He stroked him, over and over, his fingers gliding over him.

"Come on, Randy, let go."

And then he was flying. He came as Sean continued to stroke him. He shuddered with his release, shouting Sean's name as his orgasm moved through him. When he was coming down, Sean thrust into him one last time and came again, his long, loud groan one of the most erotic things Randy had ever heard.

Moments later, they collapsed on the bed. Sean moved away and went to the bathroom. When he came back, he surprised

Randy by joining him back on the bed. He wrapped an arm around Randy's chest and snuggled in closer behind him.

"I'm not good at relationships," Sean said out of the blue.

He let that bit of information sink in. "I didn't ask for one."

"Yeah, but I want to get it out of the way. I made that mistake once, and it ruined a good partnership."

Randy had heard. The moment he had been assigned to work with Sean, everyone had warned him away. Everyone had said that Sean was a man who didn't know how to commit, but Randy didn't give a fuck. He wasn't any good at relationships either. He turned to face him.

"I don't do relationships well either. Right now, let's just see where it goes, but we are both free agents. You want more, you tell me."

Sean nodded and again, the smile that curved his lips sunk into Randy's soul. Sean leaned closer and brushed his mouth over Randy's.

"I'd say I was ready for round three, but I feel like I need another shower."

Randy smiled and slid from the bed. "Sounds like a plan."

Sean followed him, and Randy thought it was a pretty good start. He'd worry about tomorrow when it got there. Right now, he'd just enjoy the ride.

PROLOGUE

SIX MONTHS AGO

*S*ean Kaheaku padded barefoot down the hallway, keeping his back against the wall. He was careful to avoid making any noise. There was no reason to alert anyone in the penthouse that he had arrived. If the package he had been sent to steal wasn't there, he could disappear without an issue.

When he reached the door to the room, he took hold of the door handle. A slight twist told him it was locked.

Dammit.

Of course it was locked. It was the way this job had gone. After missing his first flight, he'd ended up showing up twelve hours later than he had planned. Still, he was a day early, but Sean had hoped to get done faster and get out of Thailand. He wasn't well liked in some corners of Bangkok.

With deliberate moves, he pulled out his kit, picked his favorite tool. He squatted down and got to work. Why was he even doing this? He got a message from Lassiter telling him to get this package. He heard the click of the door unlocking. He slipped his tools back into his pants pocket. With a quick look down the hall in each direction, he twisted the doorknob and opened the door.

It opened slowly, and he found a completely empty room.

He frowned. There was an open window with wind billowing the sheer white curtains. Other than trash, nothing remained. It looked as if no one had lived there for months. He stepped into the room, making sure to keep his attention trained for any little sound. He walked over to the window and looked out. Nothing… just the quiet stillness of the night.

Fuck.

What now? He had been so sure that the package would be there. Lassiter had paid him to make sure. This is why he hated working alone. If Jaime and Randy had been with him, they could have used all their contacts to ensure the best results. But, for some reason, Lassiter had wanted only him on the job; and when someone pays you ten thousand for a quick pick up, you just do it. At least in his business you did. Lassiter had been mysterious and, well, weird…even for Lassiter. He'd said it was important for Sean to be the one to get the job done because for some reason, his boss thought Sean would benefit the most.

A creak sounded behind him. He turned to confront the threat, but he was too late. He saw nothing but a piece of wood that came rushing toward him. He had no time to prepare for the smack. A sharp brutal crack to his skull left him dizzy, the room spinning around him. Pain exploded then filtered out through the rest of his body. He lifted his hand and felt the spot that had been hit. His fingers touched something wet and warm. Fuck, he was bleeding.

He tried to walk, blinking to gain focus. He heard another whoosh before the wood made contact with the back of his head. Then, he was falling into a deep, dark pit of nothingness.

1

Sean came awake in a rush with the knowledge of two things: he drank too much the night before, and he was not alone. The first one had to do with the bottle of bourbon he'd crawled into the previous night. The latter came from years of experience.

He slipped his hand beneath the pillow to get his gun. He found nothing but cool sheets. Unfuckingbelievable. Since his trip to Thailand, everything in his life had gone to shit. Nothing had gone right after that night. That's what he got for being greedy. One bad job with a high price tag, and he couldn't seem to shake the clusterfuck his life had become.

"You don't need to worry about that," said a familiar female voice behind him. Her English accent had faded, but he knew the tone. Jaime was pissed.

Damn, his luck was getting shittier and shittier.

He turned over and tried to keep from groaning in pain—and failed miserably. His head spun and his stomach threatened to revolt. Every inch of his body ached as if someone had beaten the living shit out of him. Even the time when he'd been "interrogated" for a week in the Philippines hadn't left him in this sorry of shape. Worse thing was he had only himself to blame for his present situation.

He blinked at the vision standing in his room. Jaime Andrews dressed as if she were Kama'aina. But then, that was something she had always been good at. She could fit in any situation. The blue t-shirt made her Pacific blue eyes stand out even more. She had tied the shirt in a knot beneath her breasts, allowing for a view of her smooth rich brown flesh. She still had the belly ring she had gotten when they had done a job in Venezuela. Her hair was up, off her neck, and he liked it that way. It always gave him better access.

"Oh, you are a right mess, Sean," Jaime said.

"What the hell are you here for, and why did you break into my house?"

"I wanted to knock on the door like a regular person. Randy decided we needed to break in."

She motioned with her head across the room and, sure enough, Randy was there. Of course Randy was there. It was the way his luck had been going lately, not to mention, Randy and Jaime had been joined at the hip for over a year now.

Shit. He couldn't catch a fucking break. The two people who meant more to him than anyone else—until that trip to Thailand — where there to see him look like an ass. His world had been turned upside down, and he hadn't wanted to pull his former lovers into the mess his life had become.

He didn't want to face them, to let them see where he had ended up.

Sean tried to sit up and found his stomach roiling. A soft trade wind blew through the opened window, bringing with it the smell of plumeria. It was a scent that never failed to remind him of Hawaii and give him comfort—until that moment. Now, the usually pleasant fragrance made his mouth water and his belly tremble. Fuck, he'd had too much to drink. He sort of remembered the night before. It came to him in flashes. Someone had been there giving him shit about drinking too much. Del—that's who it had been. He'd appeared at Rough 'n Ready and dragged him out of the club. The memory of Del's voice as he yelled at him on the drive home pounded through Sean's head. Then, Sean remembered a very pregnant Ali was there, helping him to bed and telling him he would feel like rubbish in the morning.

"Whoa, I wouldn't move too fast if I were you," Randy said. He was dressed in cargo pants, a tight blue t-shirt, and his feet were bare. At least Randy could remember the rules of his house, even if they weren't sleeping together anymore. He'd been in the sun recently. The tips of Randy's hair always had turned to gold silk when he'd spent time on a beach. And, as usual, Randy looked fucking good enough to eat. Sean knew just how tasty that treat was.

That thought had him scowling. He'd moved on. He didn't need either one of them. He was independent and didn't need the pain.

"I think I know what I can handle."

Randy rolled his eyes and walked over to the open doors that led out to the lanai. Sean could hear the lapping of waves against the shore. Normally it soothed him, but today, it made him want to throw up. Everything did.

Jaime sat down on the bed. "What the bloody hell are you doing?"

He saw the concern in her eyes and heard it in her voice. Years ago he would have been thankful for it. Hell, he would have begged for it. These days, he needed to keep her far away. Jaime and Randy were his kryptonite, together they were deadly to his well-being even on a good day. The way things had been going they would probably the death of him.

"I think I'm sitting in my bed asking questions that are not getting answered."

"Oh, well, someone isn't in a good mood. Not our fault that you got pissed last night," Jaime said.

"I didn't know you were living on Oahu now," Randy said, breaking into the conversation.

Sean didn't think he needed to answer that question. With as much dignity that he could muster, he scooted over to the edge of the mattress and stood up. He wobbled a bit but recovered before he could embarrass himself.

"Oy, where are you going?" Jaime asked.

He slanted her a dirty look and decided to hit her right where it would hurt. "Be careful, Ms. Alexander, your roots are showing."

With that, he walked into his bathroom and shut the door. Closing his eyes, he drew in deep breaths as the room spun around him. Embarrassingly, he had to lean against the door or he would have passed out. His whole freaking house seemed to be built on a merry go round, or it felt like it this morning.

When he opened his eyes, he saw his reflection in the mirror. His eye was blackened. His torso was yellow and purple. Shit, what the hell had he done last night?

With a shake of his head, he decided he'd call Del later to find out what happened. Sean knew it wasn't going to be a story he would enjoy, and there was a good chance he would owe his old friend more favors.

∽

"He doesn't look that bad," Randy said.

Jaime glanced over her shoulder at him, then back out at the waves rolling in from the Pacific. The sound of the surf coming in was the only thing keeping her calm. Her nerves had been on edge since both she and Randy had realized Sean was missing from their lives. Of course, as soon as they arrived, Randy was rationalizing the situation. Men, they always stuck up for each other. Wankers.

"He looks like shit warmed over."

There was a pause as if Randy was trying to figure out what to say next. He probably was. She'd been ranting the entire time they searched for him.

"He's looked worse."

Irritation fluttered through her. How could he not understand? The man they both loved had just dropped off the face of the earth, then appeared in Hawaii acting completely out of character. There was something wrong and not something little. This was cock up your life kind of horrible.

"Maybe after a job. Not when he's been lying around like some kind of slacker. Just what the hell is that about anyway? He has never been a man who liked to waste time."

"Well, it's not a bad place to do his laying about. I wonder where he got the money for this?"

Jaime looked around the grounds below and knew something was really wrong. This was a house that would be featured on Hawaii Five-O where a socialite might have been killed. The furnishings had been masterfully chosen, and not by Sean. He'd like finer things, but he had no sense of style. The colors, the styles, they all looked as if someone had spent time and money to perfect the look. That definitely wasn't Sean. And, she knew one thing for sure; this had taken money. Sean had always had money, but he hadn't had this kind of money. The house was four million—at least. The way real estate prices had been ballooning on Oahu in the last couple of years, it was probably going for a lot more. That kind of money did not just plop down in your lap.

She knew the last few years, Sean had been playing fast and loose with his jobs. Getting involved with Lassiter was one of the worst decisions Sean had ever made after they split up. Randy and Jaime had walked away from taking jobs with Lassiter, partially for personal reasons, but also because Lassiter had made some dubious connections lately. Sean had kept working for him. It was his involvement with the bastard that had been Sean's downfall—or so they heard. Both Randy and Jaime had done jobs with Sean that were sketchy, mainly because they had wanted to protect him. Knowing he had gone on a job by himself, then disappeared off the edge of the earth had worried her. Subsequently…as the months had rolled by, and they didn't hear anything about him…both she and Randy had started to worry. They couldn't really put the call out for him because it might cause him issues, so they had sifted through the evidence. It had been long and painstaking, but they had finally found out what the hell happened.

Burned. As in, no connections, no protection…ruined in their business. He was considered a security risk, thanks to Lassiter—another man who had let her down more than once.

The race to find him overtook their every thought. She knew that Sean would be an ass and say he didn't need them, but he did. Burned in their world was ten times worse than being dead. At least dead you knew the pain was over.

"Babe?" Randy asked. He was worried about her. She had been a bitch on a mission from the moment they had found out.

"He's not working, we both know that."

Sean was always resourceful, but the massive mansion on Oahu was beyond his means. Not to mention the Jag and the pimped out Escalade in the driveway. There was something very wrong going on with Sean, and it wasn't all about his burning.

Randy stepped up behind her, slipped his arms around her waist and pulled her back against him. She took comfort in the warmth he offered her. He was a calming influence.

"He's okay. We'll figure out what's going on."

She sighed and let the worries she had been holding in for more hours than she wanted to think about release. It wasn't easy. It never was when it came to Sean. He was the one person who could hurt both of them without even thinking. He never understood why the two of them kept coming back.

Wanker.

"We should have gotten here sooner."

It was Randy's turn to sigh. She had repeated that phrase over and over for the past week. "Babe, you know we couldn't. We didn't know about his burning until last week."

"We should have known."

The world of security experts—especially on their level—was a small one. Everyone knew each other and, on some days, your enemy could be your best friend. The fact that she and Randy had not heard anything was, to say the least, odd. Lassiter had not told them, but then, Jaime and he were barely speaking.

"It's weird that we had not heard anything. If he's been burned for six months, someone would have said something. Hell, Lassiter should have told us."

Just another transgression to lay at the feet of Royce. The man had been nothing but trouble from start to finish, and now he had hidden Sean's status from them. She had an idea why, but she couldn't tell Randy. Not yet.

"You heard what Ross told us," she said. "He's been hanging out here in Oahu. Lord only knows why, because he always said it was too busy for him. He preferred the Big Island."

"Let's face it. There is no Rough 'n Ready there. Of course, after his behavior from last night, he might not have a membership anymore."

Club owner Micah Ross had been furious last night, but she got the feeling he was more worried about Sean than mad at him. It was the reason he poured out all the info he had on him when they had shown up. The fights, the drinking, and the fact that something was driving him into this behavior. If an acquaintance Sean didn't know that well knew of his issues, it was definitely getting bad.

Randy shook his head. "There is something bothering him.

You know he likes to brood."

"Yes, but he has never been a drunk."

And she knew why. They both did. Control was something that was so important to Sean, and drinking to excess was something he never did. Not in all the years she had known him had she ever seen him pissed, but apparently, he had been spending most of his nights that way.

"Hey," Randy said, resting his chin on her shoulder. "We'll help him sort it all out. I promise."

She closed her eyes. Tears threatened, but she would not show it. She would not lose it. She had her dignity left—and that was something she planned on holding onto. Still, it was hard to deal with Sean who had no idea what this did to both she and Randy. When he hurt, they hurt.

"I don't know what the two of you are cooking up, but I don't need your fucking help."

Randy moved away from her to look at him. Jaime opened her eyes and turned to face Sean. He didn't look any better…and he looked so damned beautiful. From the moment she'd met him all those years ago, she had never been able to take her eyes off him. He was one of those men who just seemed to capture the attention of everyone in the room.

He'd changed clothes, pulling on a pair of loose white pants and a shirt to match. At least now she couldn't see the purple bruising that had covered his chest. Even if she didn't know what he did for a living, she would recognize the lethal grace in his movements. And sweet. He was so damned sweet, but people didn't see it in him. They only saw the player. She knew the man who could make her laugh, and who would happily feed her chocolates in bed.

It didn't excuse him for being an ass, however. She decided to lay it out on the line so Sean knew exactly where they stood.

"Let's just say that we are here for answers and we aren't leaving until we get them."

2

Randy held onto his temper. Since the two volatile people of the group had decided to argue, he figured he would be the cool-headed one. When he was the one in control of his temper that was a bad thing.

But, there was nothing he could do. From the moment he had met both Sean and Jaime, they had never really been good for each other. Oil and water. Of course, he knew it made for mind-blowing sex, and that's why neither of them had been able to move on.

Sean's lip curled in disgust. "I don't think either of you deserve any answers."

"You might not think so, but then you never did," Jaime said.

Normally, he would let them continue on, but Randy wasn't in the mood. If he didn't stop both of them right now, Randy would spend most of the next few days trying to get them to forgive each other. They both had a habit of saying horrible things when they were mad.

"Stop it both of you. We came here looking for you, Sean. When you didn't answer the phone calls—and they were for some pretty lucrative jobs—we went by your apartment in Tokyo. You were gone."

Sean's expression turned even colder. "Unless you missed the last couple of years, I don't have to answer to anyone. Not even you two."

"So," Randy said, acting like Sean had never spoken. "We came here. When you need rest, you come back to Hawaii."

Sean sighed, the sound of it so solitary. It hurt Randy's heart to hear, to know that he could do nothing to make him feel better. That bridge had been burned, and there was no hope for building it again. Sean had made sure of it—but Randy knew it all had been laid at his feet. He shouldn't have been so dismissive of their relationship, but Randy didn't believe in living in the past.

Randy pushed those thoughts away. "So, what happened?"

"I had a job for Lassiter. We disagreed on the outcome. He burned me."

Randy shared a worried glance with Jaime. Getting burned in their business didn't just hurt a person financially. Randy and Jaime knew that Sean now had a big bull's eye on his back. And there were a lot of people who would want to hurt Sean. Just in the last ten years, he knew at least two-dozen operatives who would like to see Sean suffer—before killing him.

"And then, you disappear and don't call?" Jaime asked. He could feel her irritation, heard it in her voice. But there was more. Much more. She was in pain, physically hurting by Sean's rejection. Randy trailed a finger down her spine. She was holding it together, but just barely.

Sean watched the movement, then he raised his gaze to Randy's. Nothing. There was absolutely no emotion in his eyes. To Randy, that was worse than accusation or anger.

"I didn't want to pull anyone down with me. And…I had other things to do."

His tone told Randy that Sean expected no argument. He had always been that way to a point, but he had gotten worse in the last couple of years. It was one of the reasons most of Sean's acquaintances had faded away.

"You should know better than to think we wouldn't want to know, Sean. We've been working with you for the last year and a half on jobs, then you vanish."

Sean cocked his head to the side and watched them. "Funny that it took you six months to come look for me."

Randy hated that cynical expression. There had always been an edge to Sean before, but now it was downright contemptuous. There was no room for humor or even a nasty smile. It frayed the seams of Randy's temper.

"I don't care how long it took us to find you. You should have called."

Sean's expression turned to stone. "I stopped answering to anyone the day I left the military."

Jaime opened her mouth ready to blast him, but Randy saw the pain in her expression. Sean missed it because he had turned away. She straightened her shoulders and held her head high. She wanted to fight, but she wasn't ready to. He knew that she had been put through the ringer, and while most people thought she was tough, the softer side of her was damaged at the moment.

"I can't deal with this."

He heard the defeat in her voice, but Randy couldn't help her right now. Nothing would soothe her. When Sean said nothing to her, she shook her head and walked out of the room. The desolation he had seen in her gaze stabbed him and left him bleeding. She still loved Sean—they both did, but he knew she regretted their break up more than Randy had. Sean had offered everything and she had walked away.

"She's not in the best of moods." Sean's tone was almost as if he were narrating a story. So detached and cool.

Randy flexed his hands trying to remain levelheaded. Someone had to.

"You really can't blame her. She hasn't had much sleep in the last week."

"Really?"

It was easy to hear the sarcasm in Sean's voice. Most people would chalk it up to Sean being jaded, but Randy knew better. It was a coping mechanism he used to keep people away. If he hadn't been watching Sean so closely, he would have missed the tightening of his mouth that had more to do with discomfort about Jaime than any pain he was in.

"Yes. When she heard the story last night, she wanted to come over here and find you. At three in the morning."

Sean said nothing.

"So, you don't want to talk about the issue you had with Lassiter?"

He shook his head.

"And you are just going to spend days here doing nothing?"

"I do things."

Great, now he sounded like a five-year-old. Dealing with one lover who was a hot head and another lover who was a petulant five-year-old was almost too much for Randy to take.

"Right. Like drink so much you would make your stepfather feel like an insufficient drunk."

Sean's face was expressionless. "Is there a point to this conversation?"

"Yes. We are here and we aren't leaving until you come clean. And, we are going to help you."

"I didn't ask."

Randy smiled. "Neither did I, babe. Just get used to it. Princess is probably down there complaining how you have no food in the pantry."

Before Sean could object, he closed the distance between them. Randy laid a hand on Sean's cheek. "Don't be long, because you know she gets pissed when you make her wait."

Without hesitation, he did the one thing he had been

dreaming of doing since he'd seen Sean laying in bed. Randy brushed his mouth over Sean's. The moment their lips touched, his heart sang. There was only one other person in the world who could do this to him, and she was now in the kitchen complaining loud enough to wake up the dead.

He pulled back and tried not to feel so proud that Sean looked stunned. "Hurry up, you know patience isn't her strong point."

Randy left as fast as he could without looking like a coward. He had been so close to begging and that was one thing he could not do. Would not do. Besides, it was always better if you gave Sean room to think.

∽

SEAN WINCED WHEN HE SAT DOWN ON HIS BED. HE WAS REALLY fucked up when just sitting down hurt. What the hell had he done last night? The nausea was dissipating, but the pain was intensifying. He returned to the bathroom to grab some painkillers before he had to face Randy and Jaime downstairs. If he thought it would work, Sean would order them both out of his house. The chance of that happening was next to zero.

He got a couple of capsules, popped them into his mouth. Sometimes he wished he hadn't taken the job, or fucked it up so badly. Still, he couldn't regret the consequences. Not now that he had met *her*.

His head pounded like a fucking sledgehammer. Slowly, Sean opened his eyes. He was in the same room.

He listened for a long moment and determined he was alone. When he finally decided to move, he realized he couldn't. Whoever had hit him had tied his hands and feet. It took a little bit of effort, but he finally got himself righted and leaned against the wall.

Shit. He felt like throwing up. He probably had a fucking concussion.

"Be careful there. You vomit, you clean it up."

The voice was female and young. Most people would peg it as English, but it was English with an edge. She had roots in England, but she had spent most of her time abroad. She definitely wasn't from Thailand.

He blinked and turned in the direction of the voice. She was undeniably young, but not a girl. Maybe twenty-one or two. She was watching him with green eyes, familiar eyes. He blinked again. Something danced on the edge of his memory, something that he couldn't grab on to. Then, it slipped away.

"Who the hell are you?"

She smiled. It wasn't a pleasant one. "Uh-uh. I'm not sharing with you right now."

He noticed she was holding his wallet. Thank goodness he left most of his ID back at the hotel.

"I do know you, Sean. At least, what I could find online."

It was then he realized she had a computer and a small table. "My, you are resourceful."

Another smile, just as unpleasant. "You don't know the half of it. But I'm sure you will learn."

The sound of something crashing in the kitchen brought him out of the memory. With a sigh, he decided he had left it too long. Jaime had a temper, and he wouldn't put it past her to damage things in his kitchen.

With a shake of his head, he headed out of the bedroom. Then, after grabbing his phone, he went downstairs.

"I told you I would get it for you." Randy's voice was filled with amusement. He always seemed happy, even though Sean knew better. The dark secrets of Randy's years in the SEALS were well hidden from most, but Sean knew them.

When he stepped into the kitchen, he blinked. There were bowls everywhere…and flour. It was all over the counter and the floor.

"What the fuck, Jaime?"

She offered him a snarl. "We are not all giants, Sean. You put your flour way up on top."

"I can reach it there."

She settled her hands on her ships and offered him a nasty look. "Well, I can't."

"I only have to worry about myself, so I put it where I want."

Randy chuckled. "You definitely do."

Dammit, he didn't like the way his body responded to Randy's innuendo. That bridge was burned. Sean tossed him a dirty look. "Behave."

"Why? You behave enough for both of us."

He made no comment to that. Sean knew that engaging in an argument with Randy always ended badly. Well, first would be the angry sex, then there would be another fight with months of no talking.

Sean was too old for that shit. Now, he had other responsibilities.

"We can go out for breakfast," he said. "The Hukilau Café is open."

"I didn't know you would be able to eat anything," Jaime said.

"But you felt you should cook so I could smell it? You always were sadistic."

She smiled, but there was no humor in it. "You used to like that about me."

A long-strained silence filled the kitchen. He hated this. The two people he had loved most in the world, and he couldn't talk to them. He couldn't tell them just what the hell was going on. He just couldn't.

"I have to make a quick call before we leave," he said, ignoring the shared look between his former lovers. He picked up his cell and headed to his home office. After shutting the doors, he pushed the speed dial and waited. It went straight to voice mail.

Dammit. If he didn't get hold of her soon, he'd have to make a trip over to the Big Island.

Randy had his hands full at breakfast. He remembered the little café from the time he and Sean had visited years earlier, and it was one of Sean's favorite on the island. But even that did not soothe his ex-lover. *Their* ex-lover.

There would be a time that he found this funny. He knew he would be able to look back and laugh, but it was still a little raw from his encounter earlier. It wasn't that Sean had really said anything hurtful, but the damned man could never accept help. *Ever*.

"So, you two just decided to show up on the island and look for me?" Sean asked, his tone dripping with irritation.

"Yes."

"Jesus, Sean, you disappeared off the earth. What the fuck did you expect us to do?" Jamie said. To someone who didn't know her as well as he did, other people would think she was pissed. And she was. But she was hurt. Both of them were.

"It's not like I haven't done it before."

Anger, pain, and a fair dose of temper swam in Jaime's eyes before she hid it. "Yes, you're very good at disappearing when things get tough."

Sean's mouth opened—definitely to say something nasty—but the waitress had returned for their orders. By the time they ordered their meals, she had calmed down a bit. She'd been a wreck since they'd found out Sean was missing. Both of them had barely kept it together. Worse, he hadn't returned their calls. Something Randy needed to address right then.

"You want to tell us why you have been avoiding our calls for months?"

"I was busy."

Fuck. When Sean got that stubborn tone in his voice, it would take an act of God to get anything out of him. It made him good at his job, but a pain in the ass to have a relationship with.

"Yeah, we *all* have been busy."

Sean's gaze moved back and forth between Randy and Jaime. "No comment."

"Oh, that's rich," Jaime said.

"What the hell do you mean by that?" Sean asked.

"You getting pissy with us."

Sean opened his mouth to argue; but thankfully, the waitress returned with their coffee. Randy knew that it was just the calm before the storm. Jaime and Sean had always been volatile together. Randy knew that it had more to do with their relationship in general and not the breakup.

"So, do you want to tell us what happened?" Randy asked.

"I was in Thailand. Bad job. Lassiter wasn't very happy with the result and he burned me."

Randy kept his gaze locked with Sean's. He could always tell when Sean was lying. He had a tell, which most people missed, but Randy had spent too much time staring at that face. He knew the twitch. Every time Sean was lying, his left eye twitched. Just like it did now. Dammit, he was lying to them.

"So, after all these years you worked with Lassiter and now he burns you?" Randy asked.

Sean looked at Jaime then down at his coffee. "No comment."

The repeat of his response irritated Randy, even more so because Randy knew Sean said it to irritate him. He looked at Jaime expecting her to fire back, but she didn't. She apparently found her coffee as interesting as Sean's.

"Am I missing something here?"

Sean looked up, confusion clouding his gaze. Then, he glanced at Jaime. "You never told him."

Jaime shook her head.

"Told me what?"

He had a really bad feeling. Sean was always one for payback and the confident expression on his face told Randy he had leverage—and lots of it.

"Well, love, you want to tell him, or do you want me to?" Sean asked Jaime.

Jaime said nothing, her expression giving nothing away.

"Okay, this is getting fucking old. You two have bad tempers, but I tend to kill people to get rid of my bad mood."

Jaime still wasn't saying anything, so Sean stepped in. "Amazing. I thought you two shared everything."

His stomach started to sink. "Just what are you talking about?"

"What? You didn't know that your lover is Royce Lassiter's daughter?" His lips turned up into an evil smile. "Well, now you do."

3

Fury burned a hole in Jaime's gut by the time they got back to Sean's. She had never had a more uncomfortable time with the two men, including when Sean found out Randy and Jaime were an item. Having Sean show up at her room at six in the morning had been bad enough, but finding Randy in bed with her had been horrible. If there had been an argument, she could have handled that, but there hadn't been. Sean hadn't said a word. He had walked away and shut them out. Just like he had today.

Thanks to his little bombshell, they had eaten in relative silence. Randy was rarely quiet, but while she had picked at her food, neither man talked much. Of course, he had disappeared the moment they had returned, and Randy had gone to the beach to brood. They were both going to be a pain in the ass to control.

"Why the hell do I put up with two stubborn men?"

Of course, there was no one to answer. If her father had been there, he would have told her she deserved it. And there was a part of her that thought maybe she did. She hadn't always been truthful with everyone in her life. She had always reasoned that it had been to protect herself. Growing up on the streets in London hadn't been easy, and even worse when she had hit puberty. After escaping, it became more about protecting her privacy. She never felt she would be accepted if people knew she had been orphaned. Then…it became a habit. Walking away from Sean all those years ago had hurt, but she could not accept it as a total mistake. For, if she hadn't, she would have never had Randy.

It was through him she had learned how to be more open. And because of that, both of them had realized they were missing an important person in their lives.

She sighed. Truth was, her father had been scarce for months, although that was nothing new. From the moment she found out Royce was her father, they had both been avoiding each other. They worked together, but she had made it clear she wanted no one else to know about it. Sean finding out was something very odd. Her father wasn't always the best man to do business with, but he was respectful of her wishes. Or she thought she he had been.

"When were you going to tell me?"

She turned around and found Randy standing in the doorway. Damn SEAL. He was always sneaking up on her that way, but she couldn't be mad at him. She could hear the anger in his voice, but there was a thread of hurt. It was the last thing she wanted to do to him.

"I don't know if I would have ever. It's not like he's really a father to me."

"He's *your* father."

She nodded. How did she explain something so buggered up?

Randy crossed his arms and waited. Gone was the teasing lover she was so accustomed to. This was the man she usually spent time with in the field. This man made demands, and if you didn't live up to them, he left you.

"Yes."

"Are you really going to make me interrogate you?"

He would do it too. Randy could be very gentle, but when he

was hurt, he tended to lash out. Worse, he always regretted it. It was better to just give in and talk about it.

She sighed and walked to the door. "I was raised an orphan, you know that."

"So, you were truthful about that."

She hated the tone of his voice. Randy didn't trust easily, especially after Sean and everything they had been through. It had taken her months just to gain his trust so they could work together. Accomplishing the same in their personal relationship had been almost impossible.

And now it could all be lost.

"I didn't know Royce was my father. He didn't know. He had known my mother, or who he thought was my mother. It's why he hired me, trained me." And she still owed him for that. He had given her a way out of the poverty she had been so accustomed to. "He didn't put the two things together because...well, he's Royce. You know he doesn't deal with consequences well."

He nodded. "How did you find out?"

"He found out. There was a situation...you know, the shooting."

He nodded. "And you needed a blood transfusion. That was when Sean and I were on our first mission together."

When the two men had become lovers. Of course, that had to be brought up. Today just kept getting better and better. "Yes. I almost died."

There was a beat of silence. "You said it wasn't that bad."

"That's just...I told you before I knew you well enough. I didn't want to remember anything about that job." She could sometimes still hear the noise of the explosion, knowing she had lost her target...and the man she was supposed to protect. There were times she could feel the bullet ripping through her body, tearing through her flesh.

"Even that you are Lassiter's child?"

"Especially that. I have B negative blood and I needed some. I was working that job with Royce. When he found out we had the same blood type, he started to investigate. Then, he had our DNA tested."

"He did this without telling you?"

She glanced over her shoulder at him. It still angered her that Royce had done all of it without her approval. The men in her life always seemed to be doing that. "Yes. You know the man."

He sighed. "Why didn't you tell me?"

She heard the pain, and she hated that the news had hurt him. "I didn't tell you because I didn't want to. At first, I wasn't ready to. You have this great family, and I have Royce and a mother who abandoned me. I felt…inferior."

Understanding filled his gaze. He knew just how hard it was for her to say that, and she rarely shared. It was her love for him that had made it easier for her.

"I don't know how Sean found out. Royce must have told him."

Randy sighed again, then walked over to her. He stood behind her and, without hesitation, pulled her back against him into his arms. His warmth surrounded her, as did his love. They stood that way for a very long time. She could hear the waves from the ocean and smell the salt air. It had always been easy to talk to Randy, even about things like this. He accepted her as if they were the same. Probably because Randy did see them as the same. Her background wasn't important to him.

"More than likely, Royce told him. The last year or so those two have been thick as thieves."

"Yes," she said. She thought about how secretive Royce had been in the last few months. There was something going on, something that both of them were keeping from her.

"What are you thinking?"

She smiled and leaned her head back against his shoulder. "It's nice that you know me so well. I am thinking that those two are hiding something. Royce is never off the grid for me. I haven't been able to get hold of him for weeks. The office just keeps telling me that he's on a job."

"When was the last time he was on the job?" Randy murmured.

"Exactly. Something is up, and it all has to do with what happened in Thailand."

They stood there together, silent, and she knew his mind was turning over the problem.

"We have only one option."

"And that would be?" she asked.

"Our only way of finding out is making Sean tell one of us."

She snorted. "Good luck with that."

"He's our only source. You know he hasn't told anyone else if we hadn't heard about the burning. He's lain low—well, as low as you can in a multi-million dollar house. Since we know Lassiter won't be truthful with us, we'll have to get it out of Sean."

Which was going to be a bloody pain. The man held onto so many secrets, he didn't know how to be truthful even if his life depended on it. But then again, it is one of the reasons he had survived as long as he did.

"True, but it isn't going to be easy."

Randy nodded. "Now, which one of us is going to deal with the dragon?"

SEAN HUNG UP AND FROWNED AGAIN. DAYS NOW, AND HE COULD not get hold of her. Emma knew she should be answering, but getting her to do anything was like trying to get honesty from a politician. He had no real indication that they had been found out, but his gut was telling him something was about to happen. He didn't know exactly what, but he did know that things had gone on for too long. Like with his first job with Randy, he knew something was off about the situation.

He walked over to the balcony of his room. They had been home hours, and he had avoided dealing with both Randy and Jaime. It was easy enough. He'd pissed them both off in some way. After breakfast, he had stayed in his room, working on his laptop and avoiding both of his ex-lovers.

"You were always good at brooding," Randy said from behind him.

Sean didn't glance around at him. He had been dealing with the issue of Randy and Jaime for a couple of years now, but he didn't want to deal with it in his own house. Of course, he rarely got what he wanted.

He thought he had dealt with the sense of betrayal and jealousy, but at the moment, he couldn't seem to shake it.

"No comment?" Randy asked.

He didn't answer right away. Sean wanted to make sure he didn't say something he would regret. He'd already done enough damage for the day.

"I didn't think you needed one."

"You were also good at being an asshole."

He turned to face his old lover. "I am. So why are you two here and worried about me?"

Frustration marred his pretty face. The man really was gorgeous. Just like all those years ago, he reminded Sean of a California beach hunk. There were a few more laugh lines around his mouth and those sexy wrinkles around his eyes. It wasn't fair that the man just kept getting better looking by the year.

"Fuck, I don't know. Why do you think?"

The irritation wasn't new. Sean had caused enough in the last few years, but the pain he saw was different. He didn't want to deal with it, but at the moment, Sean was at a loss on how to avoid it.

"I really don't know. It's as if the two of you think I need to be taken care of."

"Fuck, I always forget how frustrating you are."

Sean found his first real smile in hours. "It's amazing how many times you seem to forget that."

Unfortunately, Randy did not return the smile like he had in the past.

"Are you really that stupid that you don't know why we are here? Why we actually *ask* to work with you?"

They asked to work with him? That information knocked him off center and, of course, Randy picked up on it.

"Ah, so you didn't know that. All kinds of secrets coming out today.."

Sean shook his head, not breaking eye contact.

Randy's features seemed to soften, and the hard gleam in his eyes faded. "Well we do."

"Why would you do that?"

Randy shoved his hand through his hair. "You are such an asshole."

"You just said that."

Randy growled and Sean tried to ignore the arousal that spiked in his blood. "We do it because we care about you. The last few years, you've been taking too many chances. Like this job that got you burned."

"I didn't get burned." The moment he said that, he regretted it. He needed to keep up the façade, to continue on as he had the last few months. It was the only way to make sure he kept Emma safe.

"You haven't worked for months. That *is* getting burned."

Dammit, he was sick and tired of that lie. He'd built a reputation and he had thrown the match to it. His reasons were honorable, and he didn't regret them. Still, after a decade of building a status in the security business, it was difficult to deal with.

"Nothing to say? So, you are okay with letting your life go to shit?"

Anger boiled in his gut. Sean opened his mouth to fire back at Randy, but he snapped it shut. Telling Randy would put him in danger. It would also put Jaime in peril, because Randy would open his big mouth.

"What?" Randy asked.

Sean shrugged and shoved his hands into his pockets. It was the only thing he could do.

Randy stomped closer and took him by the arms to shake him. He did it with such force that Sean felt as if his teeth had been rattled. Suddenly, Randy stopped, pulled him close, and slammed his mouth down on Sean's. The kiss wasn't teasing or even sexy, but more of a statement. Randy thrust his tongue inside of Sean's. He tasted of coffee and seduction. That was all it took. His mind whirled as his body responded. Randy cupped Sean's face, deepening the kiss. He needed this. It had been months since he had even wanted another lover.

As fast as it had started, Randy moved away. They were both gulping in deep breaths of air.

"What the fuck was that about?"

Randy took a moment or two before he answered. "You were always a smart man. Figure it out."

"How do you think Jaime would feel about all this?"

Something moved over Randy's expression that Sean could not seem to decipher. Then, Randy looked back to the door. Jaime stood there, leaning against the doorjamb. Randy turned back to Sean.

"I have a feeling she's okay with it." Randy cocked his head and studied him. "No comment?"

He said nothing, because he couldn't form a syllable. His brain had shut down as hormones pumped through him. Randy trailed one finger down Sean's cheek, then along his jaw. Without another word, he joined Jaime, and they walked out of the room together.

Sean stood there, irritated, confused, and with a fucking hard-on the size of Texas. It definitely hadn't been his year.

4

Sean decided he needed something to keep his mind occupied. But, what? He tried calling the Big Island, but, again, no answer. *Dammit*, the people he cared about in his life were all driving him insane. How was he supposed to get any kind of work done as he sat around waiting for this to end? Add in Randy and Jaime arriving after his drunken night, and he really thought he deserved a gold medal for not shooting someone.

What the fuck was he going to do to get them the hell out of there? He couldn't even pretend to be doing illegal jobs. The two of them would just work harder to find out what was going on so they could save him from himself. His whole adult life felt like that. People who loved him tried to tell him how to live his life. None of them knew just what went on in his head. Worse, some of his tendencies for secrecy and rudeness came about because of those relationships. His father abandoning him, his stepfather disowning him because of his bisexuality, Jaime…then Randy to an extent.

Okay, Randy was partly his fault. After Jaime had walked away from him, Sean had gotten secretive—even for another person in the security business. He couldn't allow himself to be hurt again, so he had done everything in his power to drive Randy away. Then, when Sean had asked for more, Randy hadn't been able to give it to him.

He shook his head and went into his bathroom. He needed something to cool himself off. A dip in the pool would normally do it, but Sean wanted to avoid both of them. It's was cowardly, but it was all in the name of self-preservation. He needed to get his head screwed back on straight, and then he could face them again.

~

RANDY LED THEM TO WHAT HE ASSUMED WAS A GUEST ROOM. It's where he had dropped their bags earlier. He'd decided that asking would be a mistake. When Sean dug in his heels, he would disagree just to disagree. So, to save them all the trouble of another fight, he decided to just grab one of the rooms. He figured at some point, they would sort it out from there.

"You want something to drink?" Jaime asked.

He shook his head.

"I'm going to grab some tea and be right back up. You stay away from him and we'll sort it out."

"I'm wondering if we can actually do that."

He walked over to the balcony and looked out at the ocean. The scene below was a balm to his irritated senses. Randy hated that he'd lost his temper. It was one thing he had learned to control, but Sean always seemed to push his buttons—in more ways than one. As he studied the grounds surrounding the house, he started to wonder just how the hell Sean could afford the house, but he knew better than to ask. Part of him didn't want to know. He didn't even want to think of what his friend did for the money. Sean had always had standards, but when you are cut off from your only way of making money, sometimes a person did things they normally would not have.

"You might need to tone it down, Randy," Jaime said, breaking into his thoughts.

He glanced over his shoulder at her. "That's a turn of events."

"What?" she asked.

"You telling me to tone it down. It's usually the other way around."

She hesitated, then said, "I don't always like when you two butt heads. I'm used to Sean being loud, but you're usually so laid back."

Randy shrugged. "Being nice isn't working with him."

It never did when he was like this. Although, Randy couldn't remember when Sean had been quite this bad.

"You shouldn't have pushed him."

Randy knew she was right, and it just made him madder. Pushing Sean could always end badly for everyone involved. Granted, it didn't help that he was horny as fucking hell. Teasing Sean had left him in the same state of arousal. That just added another edge to his temper. He hated that things were like this now, but he couldn't fix what had gone wrong before. What he could do was fight for Sean.

"He needed it."

She sighed. "One of the things I have loved the most about you was that you were always so calm. But every now and then, you get all hot under the collar and I have to tell you, it makes me hot."

He slanted her a look. "Why is everything sexual to you?"

She shrugged and offered him that sexy little smile that always got to him. "Around you that is just the way it is."

He slipped his hand around her waist and pulled her closer. She pressed up tight against him, and sighed. Her breath feathered over his skin just beneath his earlobe. It was definitely a trigger point for him and she knew it. The breath was followed by her tongue.

Her scent surrounded her. Jaime wasn't a woman who wore a lot of perfume, but there was the scent of her rose soap, and then the woman beneath that. Sultry and sweet.

He turned his head to capture her mouth. It was at that moment he realized he needed this...needed to be with her. Turning, he pulled her against him, and she responded immediately. It was always like this.

He backed her off the lanai, onto the room and then onto the bed. She fell back easily. Placing his hands on either side of her head, he lowered himself on top of her. He kissed her nose, then started working his way down her body. She was wearing a t-shirt, so it was easy to yank free. Of course, she wasn't wearing a bra. She rarely did whenever they were in a tropical climate on vacation. He tossed the garment on the floor and she giggled. The sound captured him as it always did. She did not get the chance to be girly enough but when she was, it made his heart sing.

He dipped his head and teased her breasts, first licking then grazing his teeth over the tips. He then kissed down her stomach, enjoying the way her muscles quivered beneath his mouth. He untied her lava wrap, and smiled when it revealed she wasn't wearing any panties.

He dropped down onto his knees on the floor and placed a hand on each of her inner thighs. Her sex was slick with her arousal. He leaned close and slipped his tongue into her pussy. He teased her, adding first one finger, then another.

He left his fingers inside of her, but moved his mouth away. He looked up at her. "Do not come."

She moaned but didn't say anything.

"Jaime, do not come."

He watched as she struggled to open her eyes. When she finally did, she met his gaze. One little nod was all it took for him to know she was agreeing to the order.

"Hands over your head. Let me see those pretty breasts of mine." She did as he ordered and he sighed. They weren't hardcore into the lifestyle, but he really enjoyed playing like this. "Yeah. I like that. Your nipples get so fucking tight."

He moved his mouth back to her pussy. God, she tasted so fucking good. There was something so damned unique about the flavor as it danced over his tongue to his taste buds. He took her clit between his teeth and tugged. She moaned, long and loud—lust and longing shimmering in the depths of it. He relished the sound as it washed through him. It added another level to his already out of control arousal.

Over and over, he pushed Jaime to the edge of pleasure, but pulled her back before letting her fall. He was about to allow it, but he sensed someone else in the room. He pulled back and looked toward the bedroom door. Sean stood there wearing only a pair of light slacks. His chest was bare and his hair looked damp.

Randy said nothing for a long time, because he couldn't form a thought. Just seeing Sean there, seeing the way he was watching them, had his pulse hammering. It took a few more seconds to gather enough control to engage him.

"Like the view, lover?" Randy asked.

Sean said nothing at first. When Jaime looked over at Sean, she lifted one hand out to Sean.

"Come."

The simple plea crumbled Sean's resistance. He apparently couldn't say no to Jaime. He walked across the room, his steps soft but steady. When he reached them, he leaned down to kiss Jaime, then pulled back to look at her.

"You want to do this?" Sean asked, his voice soft. "I'll walk away if you don't."

"More than I want my next breath." The absolute honesty was easy to hear in her voice.

His mouth curved and he turned to Randy. "And you're okay too?"

He wanted to shout yes, but he didn't. Instead, Randy returned the smile. "Truth is, Jaime and I have talked about it in the past."

His eyebrows rose up, and he looked at Jaime, then back to him. "Is that a fact?"

Randy nodded and rose to his feet. He leaned over Jaime to brush his mouth over Sean's. Randy had meant to keep it simple and sweet, but Sean cupped his face and opened his mouth, drawing Randy's tongue into his mouth. When Sean pulled back from the kiss, his mouth curved again.

As Sean pulled back, he hummed and opened his eyes. "Damn, she tastes good on your tongue."

Sean moved away and started to undress. "Go ahead with what you were doing. You don't mind, do you, Jaime?"

She shook her head, and Randy knelt down between her legs. He slipped his fingers into her pussy again. She was wetter than before. The added attraction of having Sean join them had heightened her arousal. Randy licked her clit, then stopped when Sean returned to the bed, now completely naked. The explosion of color from the bruises just added to his roguish quality. Fuck, the man always did it to him. Even battered, Sean could turn him into a puddle of melted lust. He was already hard, his erection curving up toward his taut stomach.

Sean chuckled. "Like what you see?"

Randy looked up at him. "Yeah, but you always knew that."

"Indeed. How about, we switch places. I want a taste of that sweet pussy."

Randy agreed and moved out of the way. Sean took his place.

Sean squatted in between Jaime's legs and leaned forward. He took a long breath in and sighed it back out.

"It has been so long since I've smelled that."

Jaime had risen onto her elbows to look down at Sean.

"I think I told you to lay back and keep those hands above your head."

Sean frowned at her, then smacked her sex. "He gave you an order."

She shivered and did as they ordered.

"What a good girl," Randy said, as he squeezed her nipples in response.

Smiling, Sean lowered his mouth again, and Randy watched as he feasted on Jaime. He couldn't take his gaze off the picture they presented. Sean's golden skin contrasted against her dark brown flesh in the most delicious way. Not wanting anything in the way, Randy removed his pants, then knelt on the other side of the bed.

He kissed Jaime, long, slowly, as she moaned and jolted as Sean did something to her. Randy raised his head.

"I told her not to come."

"Ah then. I guess we should take it more slowly."

Sean set his hand on her sex, barely touching it.

"Oh, Jaime, baby, you're so wet," Sean said.

"Did that make you want to come?" Randy asked her as he looked down at her. He knew Sean was continuing to tease her. "He does have the most talented tongue. I have never had a man who knew just how to suck me off the way Sean can."

She was shuddering, he knew the need for release was pretty much taking over her every thought, but Randy wanted to push her a little more.

He looked up at Sean. "Maybe she needs a little lesson."

Sean didn't hesitate. He rose to his feet as Randy helped Jaime roll over.

"Up on your knees, love," Sean said. She did as ordered again, but he expected her to. She was shaking with her need for orgasm, and she would probably do anything just to gain satisfaction.

Sean looked at Randy; the question in his gaze was easy to

see. He wanted permission to be the one to take her. But what Sean didn't understand, not yet, was that this wasn't just for now. Instead of explaining, Randy just nodded. There would be time for that later. Sean grabbed a condom package off the bedside table. After he ripped it open, he rolled it on. He took Jaime by the hips and yanked her to the edge of the bed. Randy watched, transfixed by the scene once again. He had never had a threesome before, and having it with these two people was something he had dreamed of for years. He loved them both so much and now, watching this, it touched his soul as much as it aroused him.

With one hard thrust, Sean entered her. Jaime let out another long, hard moan.

"Damn," Sean said. He opened his eyes and made eye contact with Randy. Randy's cock jerked at the lust he saw there. "If I remember correctly, Jaime likes a cock in her mouth."

"That definitely hasn't changed." He climbed up on the bed. "Open your mouth, love."

She did so readily, sucking Randy hard into her mouth. He almost came right then and there. Soon they worked in rhythm as Sean brought his hand down on her ass. The hard smack pulled a moan from deep in her throat, and it vibrated over his cock.

"Fuck, yeah," Randy moaned. "Suck it harder, Jaime. Yeah, like that."

She knew just what to do, how to run her tongue over the tip of his dick, then back down. He slipped his fingers through her hair, then he took control of her head. She opened her throat to allow him full access. Sean smacked her ass a couple more times.

Randy thrust into her one more time before he held her mouth against him as he lost himself to pleasure. His orgasm washed over him, through him and left him exhausted. He pulled out of her mouth then leaned down. He kissed her as Sean kept fucking her, his thrusts growing with intensity. She whimpered when Randy pulled away.

"Don't worry. I'll take care of you, babe."

He slipped beneath her, as Sean kept thrusting in and out of her. Randy knew Sean was close, as was Jaime. Randy lifted his head and licked the top of her mons, then teased her clit with his tongue. As Sean continued his movements, Randy teased them both, allowing his tongue to touch Sean's cock each time he thrust. Suddenly, both of them were coming. Jaime's orgasm seemed to slam through her. She screamed out, apparently surprised by the force of it. Sean thrust twice more, then came, his long groan practically vibrating off the walls.

Randy slid from beneath Jaime just before she collapsed. Sean went with her and rolled to the side, moving them up to the pillows. Randy joined them, lying on the other side of Jaime.

Sean and Jaime were still breathing heavily.

"I don't know about everyone else, but I feel better," Randy said.

Sean lifted his head. "You're such a smart ass."

"Better than a dumb one, Sean" Jaime murmured. Sean kissed her on the back of the neck, and slipped out of her.

"I'll be right back."

He went to the bathroom, as Jaime snuggled closer to Randy.

"Well, we made the first step," she whispered.

He held her close to him and kissed her temple. "Be patient. We'll work it all out."

Randy just hoped that he could stay true to his word.

5

*J*amie sighed as she felt herself drifting off. Every muscle was warm and limber. They hadn't moved much and she really didn't want to. The cool trade winds were playing with the curtains on the lanai, and she felt as if she were floating. Jaime laid her head on Sean's chest as Randy snuggled in behind her. God, it felt good to be sandwiched between them. She had never been with two men, but she could definitely get used to it with Sean and Randy. They had wlays been able to reach something inside of her that other men could never achieve. Both of them together was a dream come true. There was something especially wonderful about having all the attention on her.

Her mind started going back to their lovemaking and she hummed. She couldn't help it. For the rest of her life, she would never forget this one moment.

"What was that for?" Randy asked as he pulled her earlobe between his teeth.

"Memories."

He chuckled and it vibrated against her back. She shivered.

"I guess we should talk about it," Sean said.

She laughed. "A little too late for that."

"No, there are things you two need to know, but I can't tell you at the moment."

She shifted her weight and rose to a sitting position. Randy groaned and leaned back against the pillows.

"Come on. I thought it was sleepy time. We haven't had a good night's rest in about three days."

Sean ignored Randy's complaining and kept his attention on Jaime's face. "I liked it better when we were just going with the flow."

"You can't tell us?"

Sean shook his head. She could feel him tense up. He was ready for them to abandon him. Or give him some kind of ultimatum. Well, there was going to be one, but she wasn't going to push him beyond what he was comfortable with. Not right now. They needed to rebuild those bridges they had all burned. It wasn't going to happen overnight, but she knew at some point, they would deal with it. For the time being, she would be careful. His reaction was partially her fault. Her refusal to take their relationship to the next level—not to mention breaking it off with him then—was her fault. She had been so bloody scared at the time, and she'd made a massive mistake. But then, maybe they had needed that break...because they definitely both needed Randy.

"You're looking serious there," Sean said.

She blinked when she realized that she had been so caught up in her thoughts that she had started to frown. Before she could respond, she felt Randy's mouth moving over her flesh. Sean must have noticed what Randy was up to, because his mouth curved. He leaned forward and licked her nipple. It tightened immediately...almost painfully.

"Always so responsive," he said, lust shimmering in his voice.

Randy shifted away from her, and Sean eased her onto her back. At that point, they attacked. Sean continued to tease her breasts as Randy kissed his way down to her pussy. She was still tender from their lovemaking, but she didn't care. Randy was damned talented with his mouth, as he proved once again. He slipped the tip between her pussy lips, and she couldn't fight the moan. Didn't want to. There was one thing these men understood, and that was pleasure. Having both of them heap all their attention onto her was a fantasy come true.

Sean moved away, as did Randy. They both slid off the mattress and stood on opposite sides of the bed. Jaime looked first at Randy, then Sean. She did not care for the gleam in their eyes.

She opened her mouth to ask them what they were up to, but Randy said, "I think you should take the lead this time, Sean. She does seem to like commands coming from you."

Oh, fuck. She pressed her thighs together at the thought. Randy was right. She liked being ordered around, and there was something about the way Sean did it.

"Off the bed, Jaime," Sean said, his smile fading as his voice took a more authoritative tone.

She hesitated, and he did not like it.

"Get off that bed right now, or I will make you pay for it."

Heat flared low in her belly. Bloody hell, she had really missed this. Randy was an excellent Dom, but there was an edge to Sean that she loved also. Between the two of them, she would probably never be able to get enough—or walk straight. They both had ferocious sexual appetites.

She did as he ordered. Each small move heightened her arousal. Her sex was pulsing, anticipating.

Sean pulled her close, and patted her ass. She quivered, expecting—wanting—a harder slap, but he didn't give it. From the curve of his mouth, she knew that he had held back on purpose. Damn him.

"Walk to the foot of the bed, then face the mattress."

She didn't hesitate this time. She walked and obeyed as ordered.

"I hate that I don't have any toys at the house. I haven't played in months," Sean murmured as he walked past her, skimming his fingers over her ass.

"We do have a few things, if you are comfortable using them."

There was a pause. "Hell fucking yeah."

They walked away and she wanted to look. Sean must have sensed her curiosity because he said, "Turn around and you will regret it."

They talked softly, so much so she could barely make out what they were saying. Every few words she would catch a phrase, but not clearly enough to know what they were discussing.

"Sounds good," Sean said. "I really like this."

She heard the crack of the belt. Fuck. They had just gotten that at the store in Rough 'n Ready the night before.

"I take it you're waiting for a spanking," Sean said. He drew out the word spanking and she shivered. "But, first, I want to make sure you deserve it."

Randy was still behind her, but she heard the vibrator. If Sean was a spanker, Randy loved to torture her with a vibrator. They were going to bloody kill her.

"Why don't you start with what we talked about, Randy?"

Randy said nothing, but he chuckled. He laid on the bed, face up, with his head by her at the foot of the bed.

"Lean forward, one hand on each side of Randy, flat on the mattress."

She complied, bringing her closer to Randy's cock. She licked her lips.

"Not yet, pet. We need to make sure you earn the right to suck on our cocks."

The temptation was almost too much to bear. She closed her eyes and waited.

"No. Keep your eyes open and look at Randy's cock."

She did, and then Randy pressed the vibrator against her sex.

"Now, remember, your orgasms are ours to give you. You do not come without permission."

She said nothing, but Sean asked, "Do you accept this?"

"Yes, sir."

The moment she said it, Randy dipped the head of dildo into her pussy. It was just enough for the vibrations to jolt her clit. He moved it further in and she hummed.

"Oh, you were right. She really likes that," Sean said, his voice deepening.

"I told you. She gets so fucking wet."

Sean leaned over her shoulder, his breath feathering over her ear when he spoke. "You like that, don't you, Jaime?"

"Y-yes."

She could barely get the word out. Randy kept moving the vibrator deeper, and she could barely hold back her orgasm. Sean tugged on her ear, and licked it before moving onto the bed. Randy slowed down the vibrator, but took one of her nipples into his mouth. The dual torture was almost too much to bear.

"Fuck."

"Oh, such a dirty mouth," Sean said, dark amusement filling his voice.

He wrapped his hand around Randy's cock, and she watched as Sean stroked Randy. Sean turned his head and looked at her as he lowered his mouth to Randy's cock. He licked up the underside, then took the shaft into his mouth. She watched, unable to look away as Sean started to deep throat Randy. It brought a moan from Randy, which vibrated over her nipple then through her body.

Randy tore his mouth away from her nipple. "Fuck, yeah, that feels good. Yeah, fuck. Fuck, just like that."

Sean continued working him over as Randy held the vibrator with one hand, then molded his other on the back of Sean's head.

It was one of the sexiest things she had ever seen. She couldn't look away, even if Sean had ordered her. Then, Sean pulled back, giving Randy's cock one last long lick before he moved off the bed.

"Liked that, didn't you, princess?" he asked, his voice was deeper, darker.

"Yes, sir."

He licked his lips and hummed. "Randy has always been a tasty treat." He smiled. "And you didn't look away like a good pet."

Randy chimed in. "She is fucking wet too. I'm amazed she hasn't come yet."

"Oh, that deserves a little reward."

He picked up the belt where he had left it on the bed and moved behind her. Randy started to lick and tease her breasts again, turning up the vibrator another notch.

The moment the belt hit her ass, she jolted and almost came. She dug her fingers into the sheets, forcing herself not to come. He hit her again; the sharp sting of the belt left her flesh hot. Jaime closed her eyes in anticipation of the next smack, but it didn't come.

"I told you to keep your eyes open and on Randy's cock."

It took a second or two, but Jaime forced herself to do as he ordered. He smacked her with is bare hand as a reward.

"Damn, your skin is hot."

He moved back again and hit her three more times. By the time he was done, every nerve in her body was singing. She was at the edge about to come, but Randy removed the vibrator, then moved away from her, slipping off the mattress. He joined Sean behind her.

"Damn, babe, I bet you loved that," he said as he skimmed his fingers over her ass. The light touch was enough to tease her more.

"You did so well, Jaime, so I think you need another even

better reward," Sean said, as he took her hand and moved her away from the bed. "Care for a ride, Randy."

"Fuck yeah," Randy said, slipping onto the bed. He had a condom on, ready to go as Sean helped her up on the bed. It was hard to do, because she was so damned close to coming, she could barely think properly. Her legs and arms were shaking.

Jaime straddled Randy, sliding down on his cock, and humming as she did.

"Oh, yeah, I know what it feels like having his cock inside of you."

She opened her eyes and looked at Sean, who knelt beside them on the bed. She kept her gaze on his as she rose up then lowered down on Randy's cock. She did that a couple more times, watching as Sean stroked his own shaft as he watched them. Then, he moved closer to Randy's mouth and held it out.

"Want a taste?"

"I think that deserves another 'fuck yeah,'" Randy said as he eagerly opened his mouth to take Sean in. Again, she was transfixed by the sight. Sean rested his fists on his waist as he jettisoned in and out of Randy's mouth. She continued to move, her orgasm shimmering so close.

"You can come when you want to, love," Sean said. It was all she needed. Her release tore through her, pulling a scream from her as she convulsed.

"Ah, yeah," Sean said, and he thrust into Randy's mouth one last time. He held still. He pulled his cock out then lay down beside Randy. He leaned forward and stroked her clit. She thought she was done, but as Randy moved his cock in and out of her, and Sean stroked her, she felt the delicious pressure build again.

"Shit," Randy said. "Fuck, yeah, that's it. Stroke her. I want to feel her come again. All those fucking muscles on my cock. Yeah, that's it," he said, as another orgasm jolted her.

"Fuck," Randy said, as he grabbed hold of her hips and started to thrust up harder and harder, then with one last shout, he thrust into her and gave over to his orgasm.

She collapsed on him just moments later as Sean lay down next to them. Sean slipped his fingers through her hair; rose up to kiss her, then leaned down to kiss Randy.

"Now, we can sleep," Sean said.

"You both definitely made sure of that," she mumbled.

Randy chuckled as he stroked her ass with a sweet caress, soothing the tender skin. With Sean's arm over her and Randy, she laid her head on Randy's chest and fell asleep.

6

Sean splashed water on his face to wake himself up. He awoke from a dream he couldn't remember, but he knew it had to do with Emma. She had been in some kind of danger, and he remembered running through hallways searching for her. She had been screaming for him. His pulse still hammered in his throat, and it was made worse by the fact that he couldn't get hold of her.

Where was she?

After the panic had dissolved, he knew he wouldn't get back to sleep. So, he'd slipped out of bed and went back to his own room to clean up.

As he dried off his face, he realized there was a reason people had been worried about him. He'd never had an issue with his weight, but he had dropped at least ten pounds. It showed in his face. Damn, he had to get this crap cleared up and get on with his life. Too many times he had put it on hold; but now, he wanted a future. He wasn't sure where the three of them were going. Thinking about it would lead to hoping and, at the moment, Sean just didn't have the energy to do that. Not with what was hanging over his head at the moment. Before he took on two more people in his life, he needed to protect the one who meant more than anyone else at the moment.

He went to his closet as the memories of his first days with Emma washed over him.

"Get in the car," he said, as he glanced from side to side, making sure no one had followed them. Of course, the young woman ignored him and disagreed with him.

"I don't understand why I need to go with you. I was doing fine on my own."

He heard the irritation in her voice, but there was something else.

"You were doing so well that you were kidnapped." Still, she didn't move. "Let me put it this way, sweetheart. Get in the car, or I put you in the car."

She studied him for a long moment, then she did as he ordered. Once they were both situated in the car, he started it up.

"It would save a lot of time, if you would just do as I say," Sean said.

She narrowed her eyes, but he ignored her as he pulled out into traffic. He needed to contact Lassiter and find out just what the hell was going on. Then he needed to find out just who the hell this tiny bundle of energy was to him. There had to be a reason he had been requested for the job.

"Do you even know where you are going?"

He didn't respond. He focused on driving them through the insanity of Bangkok traffic. One wrong move and they would be dead.

"Sean?" she demanded.

"What?"

"Do you know where you are going?"

"The airport. Then we are getting out of here."

She said nothing as he flew through another red light. He didn't know how much time they had before they would go unnoticed.

"Why would I go to the airport with you?"

"I have a feeling the guys who kidnapped you were not doing it to get to know you. I have a private plane I chartered, and we are getting the fuck out of Bangkok."

She opened her mouth to complain again, he was sure, but he stopped her.

"Listen, I am going to get us to safety. Then, from there you can decide if you want to tag along or not. But, I can guarantee you, those men weren't going to continue to play nice, if they had been. Soon, you probably would have been sold off."

"Oh, I doubt that."

"Why would you say that?"

"My mind is worth more on the open market than my body."

Sean shook his head as he stepped into a pair of loose fitting pants. The woman was a handful, but then, she had been worth it. He would put up with all the trouble that had exploded in his life just for her. None it had been her fault and Sean didn't believe in killing the messenger.

He made his way down the hall as quietly as possible. He stopped at the doorway to the guest room and looked in. Randy and Jaime lay in bed, their bodies entwined. It was so hard to force himself to walk away. He wanted to slip beneath the sheets and snuggle up to the two of them. But, he also knew he had unfinished business before he could commit to anything.

He turned away from the temptation they presented and walked to his home office. He'd set the office up when he realized he needed something with higher security than he could get from the average Wi-Fi. Of course, Emma had done all the work securing the lines. The woman was too smart for her own good. But, like most people like her, she couldn't see the forest for the trees. And those trees tended to fall on her before she noticed what was going on.

After turning on his desk light, he decided to check on a few things and try to call Emma again. They hadn't talked in days, and while she had a habit of disappearing from time to time, she always caught up with him a few days later. She knew he would worry.

He settled down in the chair behind the desk and started up

his computer. He rolled his shoulders and realized that he was sore in places he didn't know he could be sore in. He had always had an active sex life, but maybe he had been slowing down in the last year. It made sense with what had been going on, but still, he was starting to feel old. Of course, he had never had a threesome before, and both Jaime and Randy had been the two lovers who had challenged him on every level.

He rested his head against the back of the chair and closed his eyes. Sean didn't know what would happen after this was over, but he knew that he was never going to be the same. There, in the office alone, he could admit that he wanted more, but what? How did he ask the two of them to stay around when his life was such a fucking mess?

Opening his eyes, he leaned forward and keyed in his password. As he waited for everything to load, he realized it had probably been well over thirty-six hours since Jaime and Randy actually slept. He sighed. No wonder they had passed out. It had been hard to force himself to leave the bed, but with both of them sleeping, now was the best time to do some research.

He checked his email and found nothing. Not even one of Lassiter's strange emails from fake names. It was really starting to worry him. Lassiter was one sneaky bastard, but the last few months, he had kept in contact, in his own way. The fact that he was universally absent from everything was really, really bad. He checked a few more emails and realized one of this old buddies from MI-6 had emailed him. He scanned the email and realized things were finally moving forward. It looked like the beginning of the end of the nightmare that had started six months earlier, but he didn't want to get his hopes up.

With that on his mind, he picked up his phone and dialed Emma. Nothing. It just rang and then went to voice mail.

"Emma, this is Sean. The only person who calls you. Things seem to be shifting and we need to discuss strategy."

He hung up and sat back in the chair. His nerves were

stretched to the limit, but he couldn't show it. Not to Jaime and not to Randy. Hell, he couldn't really let anyone know what was going on. If Lassiter had been picked up, there was a good chance Sean's moves could definitely tip off his captors. That would put his life in jeopardy.

Shutting down his computer, he decided to grab a shower before he made it back to bed. Maybe it would clear his head and give him a direction for what to do next.

Perhaps, he could possibly figure out what the hell to do about Jaime and Randy.

∼

Royce Lassiter made his way down the street in the seedier side of Paris. It was one of those areas most tour guides would tell you to avoid, but he felt pleasantly at home. He'd grown up in an even tougher part of London, so it wasn't as if he didn't know what to expect. There was a good chance he was going to get mugged, but he would welcome that. Being hunted wasn't something he wanted to ever experience again.

Fuck, he was tired. His head pounded due to his lack of sleep, his back was killing him, and dammit, he smelled as if he had been sleeping in a pile of rubbish that was three days old. Every time he caught his scent he wanted to vomit. He was too old for this shit. This was a game for a younger man. He knew because he had been that younger man at one time. In the years he worked for MI-6, he did things most people would call…questionable. He had lived a life that most people would only dream of, and after a successful career with the government, he had started his own corporation that had made him richer than he had ever dreamed of being.

And it was all in jeopardy.

If this situation wasn't because of Sean, he would have just bailed, but he owed his old friend. Royce knew that part of this was his fault. He had taken chances in the last few years and some of that had to do with making money, and other times it was all ego. But now, he would set it all right, fix things. He needed to make things up to Sean, plus, he had to make sure his daughter was safe and sound.

He came upon a little deli that was getting ready to close. He needed to eat and get a message to Sean. Things had gone to shit in the last thirty-six-hours. Hell, even the connections he could always count on weren't coming through.

As Royce approached the door, he heard something behind him. Knowing he was stuck, he turned to face the threat. He never saw a face. No sound was made, but he felt the burn of the bullet as it passed through his shoulder. He lost his footing and fell back. He hit the sidewalk hard, first with his ass, then his back and finally his head.

He blinked as his vision wavered.

"Come on," someone said, as two men grabbed him. He couldn't really place the accent, but he was sure it was Eastern European. "There is someone very interested in meeting you, Mr. Lassiter."

Before he could ask who it was, he felt something hit the back of his head and then nothing at all.

7

Randy jerked awake, thinking he heard something. He lay there quietly, wrapped around Jaime as she snoozed. He listened for a long moment, and realized he heard water running. When he looked on the other side of Jaime, he saw Sean was gone.

As gently as he could, he slipped away from Jaime and off the bed to go find Sean. Randy knew Sean would have issues, and Jaime and Randy had talked about them. Arriving as a couple—as they had been for over a year now—certainly would make Sean think he was the outsider. Both he and Jaime knew they had a lot of work with Sean to get him to understand their position. They wanted him in their lives, and they needed him to understand that. But, as Jaime had pointed out, if they said that to begin with, Sean would disagree because…well, that's the way Sean was. At least now he was, partially due to his involvement with both Randy and Jaime. They had a lot to make up for.

He knew without looking, Sean wasn't in the guest bathroom. Of course he wasn't. He had probably retreated to his own room wanting some space between them. Sean would always be moving away from them until they made him understand. Randy

could be patient to a point. Sneaking away after making love…
that he would not allow.

Moving down the hall as quietly as possible, Randy crept into
Sean's room. He'd left the door to the room open, along with the
bathroom door. Light spilled into his bedroom, along with a fair
amount of steam. Randy knew from past experience Sean was
trying to think something through. The man always did his best
thinking in the shower.

He padded quietly to the doorway and watched from there. It
had been a long time since he'd had time to watch Sean like this.
He was a creature of habit, a man who loved water, and damn, he
looked good with it sliding down his body. Randy's cock hardened as he watched Sean soap up a massive sponge then slide it
over his flesh. Sean was definitely aroused and, *dammit*, Randy
loved watching him move that soapy sponge over his cock. Soapy
water dripped from the tip of Sean's dick. Fuck, even with the
few pounds he'd lost, Sean was a man who would tempt just
about any man or woman in the vicinity. Knowing just how
talented he was in bed made it even harder to ignore him.

Sean must have sensed him there. He glanced over his
shoulder.

"Hey."

"What are you doing in here all by yourself?" Randy asked.

"I didn't want to wake you two."

That might have been true, but Randy knew there was something else there too. He was trying to keep himself separate, but
Randy wasn't going to allow that. Without waiting for an invitation, Randy opened the door to the shower and stepped in.

Sean's gaze moved down Randy's body. Just that one little
look had Randy's cock jerking.

"I see you still live up to your name," Sean said as his mouth
curved.

Fuck. All the man had to do was give him a look and say a few
words, and he was ready to suck him off. It had been that way

from the first. Both of them had forgotten how much they wanted—needed—each other. It's why they screwed up their relationship before.

Moving closer, he pressed against Sean, gyrating his hips so his cock caressed Sean's ass. He was wet and so fucking sexy; Randy didn't know how he could ever have walked away from him. Add in the sweetness he hid from other people and he was too much to resist.

"Hmm," Sean said as he dropped the sponge and leaned against the wall. The water hit Randy, making both of their bodies even slicker. Randy reached around to wrap his hand around Sean's cock. Randy stroked him a few times before the door opened behind them. They both turned around to find Jaime standing there wearing her favorite red kimono.

"So, a girl gets a little rest and boys run away to play?"

Randy chuckled. "I thought you needed rest."

She shook her head and undid her robe, letting it fall to the floor. She stepped in the shower.

"By all means, continue," she said with a smile.

Randy looked at Sean, who met his gaze. He released Sean's cock and turned him around. Backing Sean up against the wall, Randy ignored the water and kissed him. He put everything he had been feeling in the last few moments into the kiss. Sean responded immediately, his tongue thrusting into Randy's mouth as he reached around to grab his ass. Sean pressed them closer, their cocks sliding against each other.

"Oh, my," Jaime said, her voice a bit breathless.

Sean tore his mouth away from Randy's and looked at her. "This doesn't bother you that we were in here by ourselves?"

She shrugged as her gaze moved down their bodies, then back up to meet Randy's. She looked at Sean again.

"No. No more than it would if Randy had found me bent over the bathroom counter as you fucked me. Share and share alike."

Sean hesitated, then he groaned and turned back to Randy.

This time, Sean unleashed the hunger he had been feeling, and it hit Randy like a hurricane. Randy tilted his head to one side to allow Sean deeper access to his mouth.

When Sean finally pulled back, they were both breathing heavily. They turned together to look at Jaime. She had her hand between her thighs stroking her pussy.

"Now, who gave you permission for that, Jaime?" Randy asked.

"Get that hand off our pussy," Sean said.

She hesitated, then relinquished to their command.

Randy looked at Sean and he nodded, giving Randy the lead this time. Fuck, playing opposite of Sean with Jaime was beyond anything he could have dreamed of. Jaime turned him on, but the other level was enjoying her sensual torture with another man.

Jaime was frowning at them as she tried to close her legs, but Randy shook his head.

"Nope. Keep those legs wide. Sean and I like looking at our pussy. And put your hands on the bench beside you."

She did as he ordered. Water was sluicing down her body, dripping from her nipples. Sean moved foreword to lick the water from one of her nipples.

"I always thought you were a voyeur," Randy said. "Now I have confirmation."

Sean straightened and waited for Randy to make the next command. They hadn't really spoken of how to handle the situation with two Doms in the mix. It was as if they could tell what the other was thinking.

"Jaime," Randy said. "Open that sexy mouth of yours."

She did and he nodded to Sean. He stepped forward and she took his cock in her mouth. Randy took her hand and wrapped it around his cock. She sucked Sean over and over as she slid her hand over Randy's cock. The water made it easy for her to do what was needed. Sean stepped back and let Randy closer. She took Randy into her mouth and he almost came. Sean was watching; his gaze transfixed on what Jaime was doing to him. The dual assault on his senses almost had him coming. But, he didn't want that. He wanted to go beyond what they had done before. He pulled back, and Jaime moaned in unhappiness.

"Ah, I like hearing that," Randy said as he bent down to kiss her. Sean did the same as they turned off the water and stepped out of the shower. They took their time drying her. Sean took her front and Randy took her back.

"I bet you know this, Sean, but she does like to be touched and teased."

"Yeah, she has always been one of my most responsive lovers. Aren't you, Jaime?"

He leaned down and kissed her and Randy watched. Hell, all of them were probably voyeurs in their own way. As he watched Sean deepen the kiss, he remembered the one Sean had given him in the shower. It aroused him on a whole other level.

When they were done drying off, he shared a look with Sean. "Got some in the linen closet."

Randy shook his head as he smiled.

"You two are starting to scare me," Jaime said.

Randy turned her around and kissed her. "Good," he said, as he raised up he swatted her ass. He looked at Sean, who had pulled out two condoms and some lube. "Ready to try us both, love?"

She looked at him, then back at Sean and nodded.

Randy jumped onto the counter, and took a condom from Sean. He handed it to Jaime and said, "Put it on."

She did as he ordered, taking her time as she rolled down the length of him. Randy curled his toes and tried his best not to show his reaction. Of course, it did no good. Jaime and Sean always knew just how to entice him. Sean chuckled.

"She likes to be teased, but she definitely likes to be the teaser herself."

Jaime turned around and waited for the order. Aw, damn, she

was so fucking sweet. This connection was what they had all needed.

"Do the same to Sean."

She took the condom wrapper, and gave Sean the same treatment, but she was worse. Taking her time, she slid the condom down, pressing her thumb over the top of it. Sean shuddered in response.

"Of course I like to tease," she said. "It always makes both of you so hot, you fuck my brains out."

He looked over her shoulder at Randy. "She's picked up your dirty mouth."

Randy chuckled. "That she has."

Sean picked her up and set her on Randy's lap, then he leaned forward and licked her pussy. He dipped his tongue down Randy's cock, to his sac, then back up to Jaime's pussy. He did that a few more times before dipping his tongue between her pussy lips.

Jaime moaned and leaned her head back on Randy's shoulder.

"Oh, yeah, baby, you like that, don't you?" he asked.

She nodded her head as he slipped his hands around to her breasts. Her nipples were hard, and he knew they were sensitive. She always responded so readily when he pinched them, and this time was no different. Sean stood up. He kissed Jaime first then he kissed Randy. The taste of Jaime's arousal danced over his tongue. When Sean pulled back, he took the lube and spread it over his index finger. Watching them both, he eased his finger into Jaime.

"Randy?" he asked. Without the words, he knew what Sean was asking. He lubed his finger up and joined him. Fuck, she was tight with both their fingers up her ass.

"Oh, oh," she said. Her body shook like she had been jolted with electricity.

"Just say your safe word, if it is too much," Randy said.

She nodded but didn't use it. Instead, she released a breath and relaxed as they worked in unison. Sean leaned forward and kissed Randy again. They turned to her and brought her into the kiss.

"Fuck, yeah," Jaime said.

Now, they were moving their fingers in and out of her ass, increasing their rhythm and she was moving with them.

"Oh, yeah, like that," she said. They both realized that she was really damned close to coming.

They removed their fingers, and Sean helped Randy hold her up so he could guide his cock into her ass. Slowly, he worked his way up in her. She was tight, but it definitely wasn't her first time trying anal sex. They had experimented with all things…and when they had talked about approaching Sean, they knew they would have to be ready. When he was as far as he could go into her at the moment, he nodded to Sean.

Sean took his cock and slid it over her slit.

"Oh, yeah, you like that, don't ya, Jaime?"

"Hmm," was all she could say to him. Sean pulled back and smacked her pussy. She jerked, tightening her anal muscles around Randy's cock.

"Fuck, do that again, Sean."

He did and both Randy and Jaime moaned together. He did it once more and Jaime screamed in delight.

Sean positioned his cock and slowly worked it into her pussy. As he did, Randy felt the pressure build against his cock. With both of them in her, it was incredibly tight.

"Oh, God," she said.

"Remember…" Sean didn't finish. He groaned as he made his way all the way inside of her. "Remember…to…use your safe word if you need it."

"She feels like fucking heaven, doesn't she?" Randy asked. Sean opened his eyes and nodded.

They both started to rock in and out of her, working into a

rhythm that worked for all of them. Sean dipped his head to tease her breasts with his mouth as Randy kissed her neck.

As their tempo increased, Sean lifted his head and kissed them both again. Randy reached around and stroked her clit.

"Come on, Jaime, come for me. We want to feel you come while we are inside of you."

That was all it took. "Oh, Randy. Sean. Fuck."

She jerked against them both as she came. But without even discussing it, they both kept moving, teasing her. They made her come again, and again, and again. She was chanting their names over and over by the time Sean thrust into her one last time. He leaned forward, kissing Randy as he came. When Sean recovered, he pulled out of Jaime, then moved her feet up to the counter.

"Ride him," he said as he started massaging her clit.

"No, I can't handle another one," she said, her voice breathless.

Sean smacked her pussy. Her ass tightened on his cock again. Fuck, it was the most exquisite torture he'd ever felt. Sean smacked her sex again, but waited for Randy to say what needed to be said. He was in charge and Sean was still giving him the lead.

"You will ride me, Jaime, or we will make sure you get so fucking horny with no relief, you'll do anything we ask."

Sean leaned down and started to lick her as she lifted up and down on Randy. Again, she tightened around his cock and that was all it took.

"Oh, yeah, fuck," Randy said, as he felt his orgasm approach. The flick of Sean's tongue over his sac sent Randy up and over into his orgasm. As pleasure took over Randy's every thought, Sean helped Jaime, taking her by the hips and guiding her up and down as she rode Randy through his orgasm. As Randy was crashing down from the high of his orgasm, Sean leaned down once more and took her clit into his mouth. Her last orgasm slammed through her, pulling a surprised scream that echoed off the walls of the bathroom.

Moments later, they made it into Sean's bedroom, all of them collapsing onto the mattress. He had never been through anything so thrilling or exhausting. Jaime lay between them, just as they had made love just minutes earlier.

Randy kissed the back of her neck. "Thank you, Princess."

Sean hummed and kissed her mouth. "Yes, that was amazing." He then leaned forward to kiss Randy. That inclusion, the way he made sure they both felt part of the whole…that was the sweet side of Sean. As Sean pulled away, Randy saw the emotion, the need right there in Sean's gaze. He tempted him on so many levels, but more importantly, just like it had always been with Jaime, the connection spoke to his soul.

Sean offered him a sleepy smile as he settled his head on the pillow beside Jaime. Damn, the man was getting to him again.

As Randy drifted off to sleep, he hoped that they had made another step forward, because he didn't know if either he or Jaime would be able to take the step back.

8

By early afternoon, Sean was ready to give up. He couldn't seem to get hold of Lassiter, and with Emma ignoring his phone calls, his worry increased with each hour. She was a tough little woman, but she had a lot of people who wanted to hurt her to get back at him. He should have never put her on the other island, but it was the best option at the time. She was living off the grid, well, as off the grid as she would go. No way anyone knew who she was—or so he thought.

One good thing about the situation was that Devon Stryker had given him use of his company's private jet. It would make it much easier to steal Emma from the other island and bring her over.

He'd contact Crysta and Eli to see if they could check on her, but he knew it was a big time for the Ranch on the Big Island. It was the annual rodeo time that Kaheaku Ranch threw each year. Either one of them would jump to help, but with Crysta pregnant with their first child, Sean couldn't bring himself to put her in danger.

He couldn't go himself. First problem were the two people he could trust with just about everything else in his life: Randy and

Jaime. They would want to know what was going on if he had to hop over to the Big Island. He would have to tell them, but he wanted Emma with him when that happened. The closer she was, the easier it was going to be to make both of them disappear if this entire plan blew up in their faces.

Second problem was he had a target on his back. True, he was relatively safe in his house, but if he went out in public with Emma, they would become targets. Her death would be punishment before he was killed.

Sean knew he needed help, and the only person he could trust was going to be a pain in the ass about it, and for good reason.

He dialed the number. His friend picked up on the first ring.

"Delano," he said, his voice heavy with sleep. As the head of Task Force Hawaii, Del kept strange hours.

"Del, I need help."

He grunted. That wasn't a good sign.

"You didn't say that a couple of nights ago."

Mortification filled him. During his adult life, he refused to be a drinker like his stepfather. He had avoided it for years for that reason. The fact that he had lost it and gotten drunk—then went out in public was bad enough. Taking a swing at a friend was just a big fat cherry on top of his shit sundae.

"I owe you for that. I definitely could have hurt someone on my way home."

He sighed, then it sounded like he stood up and started walking. "Especially yourself, man. You got to stay off the liquor."

"I am off. Don't worry. Haven't had a drink since that night." Even now the thought had his stomach turning over. "Now, about this favor…"

"I expect a nice steak and lobster dinner."

He didn't hesitate. "You got it."

"How about an introduction to that sexy Jaime I heard was looking for you the other night?"

Sean could tell from Del's tone that he was just joking, but he couldn't hide his animosity at the request.

"No."

He chuckled. "Okay, what do you need?"

"How does flying over to the Big Island on a private jet sound?"

There was a pause. "This isn't illegal, is it?"

"Nope, on the up and up. I need you to get a package for me."

"Is that a fact?"

"I have a friend on The Big Island, and I can't get hold of her."

There was another pause. "You want me to kidnap a woman for you?"

This time, there was a thread of anger in his voice. That is one of the reasons Sean knew he could trust Del. Women and children always were to be protected. Not everyone in Sean's business played that way.

"No. I need you to bring her here for her safety. She might be in trouble."

"Then, why the hell don't you go check on her?"

He really liked Del, but the man was cranky. Damned cranky. And he liked to growl. He would do as Sean was asking, but he would complain while he did it. Sean couldn't be choosey, not right now.

"You know I've had trouble. I don't want to lead it to her door."

"But you want me to bring her over here? That makes no sense."

It did, and he didn't have time to deal with questions. "I want to move her to a safe house close by. Then, if we need to get out of here, Devon Stryker can make sure we get off the rock."

"Hmm. Is that the private jet I'm using?"

"Yes."

"Okay. I'll go."

Relief filtered through Sean. "Thanks. I really appreciate it. I can't trust anyone else to get her, and I know you can keep her safe."

"I'll call when I make contact."

He hung up. The man definitely didn't have the best manners; but then, Sean didn't need him for his manners. As a former Army Ranger and now head of Task Force Hawaii, Del would make sure Emma made it back to Oahu safe. That was all Sean cared about.

~

MARTIN DELANO PARKED HIS RENTAL CAR ON THE STREET AND looked at the fortress and frowned. It was pretty far off the beaten path, but that was to be expected. The Big Island had a lot of people who liked to live off the grid. If someone didn't want to be found, it was easy to stay lost. The gates were closed but, even at this distance, he could see there was no sign of life. He wanted to turn around and head back to Oahu, but he couldn't. He had promised Sean.

Resolutely, he walked up to the gate and looked more closely. He saw the curtains in the top floor flutter. Someone was in there.

He punched in the security code Sean had texted him and made his way to the front door. Since the one little flutter of curtain, he had seen nothing else. He made it to the front door and rang the bell. Nothing. He walked over to one of the windows and looked in. Suddenly, he heard a sound behind him. He turned just in time to be hit with something heavy and hard.

He blinked a few times. His nose was throbbing and blood was pouring from it. A woman was standing there with what looked like a heavy two-by-four, ready to hit him again. She was Asian and was on what women called the petite size. In his mind, she looked like she could be picked up and put in his pocket. When he didn't move, her green eyes narrowed. He started toward her, and his world start to turn. Blood slid down his face as he staggered. Fucking hell. That hit had been harder than he realized.

The woman pulled back the piece of wood, getting ready to hit him gain. He stopped her and grabbed the wood.

"Hey," she screamed.

He held the piece of wood out of reach and leaned down in her face. "You hit me with that thing again, and I will kill you."

He tried to sound as mean as he could. It didn't work on her. She lifted her knee, making contact with his groin. He bent over in pain.

"Fuck off, wanker."

She turned to run into the house. He grabbed for her arm but caught only air.

"I'm calling the police."

He took a step and almost threw up. When he spoke, he bit out every word. "I *am* the police. Sean sent me."

She stopped but didn't come back. She turned to face him but kept her distance. "Sean?"

He nodded. Fuck, he shouldn't have done that. His nose throbbed even more.

"Well, why didn't you say so?"

She asked the question as if he were stupid. And he had to be if he kept doing this kind of crap for his friends.

"The only thing that is saving you is that he asked me to do this."

She cocked her head and studied him for a moment. The longer her green gaze watched him, he felt oddly dizzy. It had to be the knock to his face because that fucking hurt.

"What would happen otherwise?" she asked.

"I would have shot you."

Her mouth twitched and something close to respect filled her expression. "I don't think my brother would like that much."

He blinked as the world shifted a bit. "Your brother?"

"Didn't Sean tell you? I'm blood."

He shook his head and immediately regretted it. It felt as if she had knocked his brain loose. "That figures, because every time I'm around him, I end up injured."

She chuckled. "Come on. I am assuming he wants you to call."

༄

The phone rang only once and Sean answered.

"How is she?"

"She's safe. She just wasn't answering her phone."

Something loosened in his chest. Damn, when had it gotten so scary being a big brother? Probably the moment she smacked him upside the head with the board.

"Give me the phone," Emma said. From the sound on the other end of the line, they were physically fighting over the phone.

"Go get bent, Taylor. I don't have time to deal with you."

Sean let loose a breath he did not know he had been holding. "Thank you, Del, I owe you."

"Yeah, you do. It might cost you more after I go see a doctor."

"The doctor? Emma didn't get hurt, did she?"

"No. She's fine; although, I still might shoot her before we leave the island. Your *sister* hit me with a two-by-four."

Sean couldn't fight the grin. "She did the same thing to me when I went looking for her."

"If you don't let me talk to him, I will post the pics I took of you online. I am sure all your wanker friends will love that. I got one when you were crying like a baby."

Del made a sound between a cross groan and a growl. "You do not have one of me crying."

Emma snorted and Sean could see her standing in front of Del with her arms crossed as she tapped her bare foot on the ground.

"Close enough, and I have a good hand with Photoshop."

"Dammit. If you don't let go, I will smack you upside the head." The struggled died off. "Fuck, I have only met one of your relatives, Kaheaku. One too many."

The phone jostled. "Give that back to me."

"Get bent yourself, Delano."

Sean couldn't help but chuckle now. He might have never wanted a sister, but damn, he really liked her now that he'd found her. "Hey, Sean. Why did you send the Neanderthal over here?"

"You weren't answering your phone. I told you to always answer."

She sighed. "Sorry. I just wasn't paying attention, and I was working on something."

He knew that her mind worked constantly, and she did have a tendency to lose track of time. "There's been some activity. I think we need you to come over here."

She didn't say anything. "I am not sure that is a good idea."

"Why?"

"I can't put you in any more trouble than you already are. Plus, if we keep our distance, we are safer."

"As I said, things have changed. It would be best if you are here. If things get bad, we will find you another place to hide. Besides, we're family. That's what matters."

"Can't I just stay here?"

"No. You need to be safe."

"I am safe here. Unless this idiot had a tail. Is this the one you told me about?"

Although he knew she couldn't see him, he shook his head. "No. Randy is here with me."

"Oh. Okay."

She said nothing else. The silence stretched, and he knew she was trying to come up with some way of convincing him to change his mind.

"Either way, I want you here."

"Sean, please, let me stay here."

He heard the desperation in her voice, knew what it was about, and felt like even more of a bastard because he had to ignore it. She was not good with change for several reasons, but he couldn't do anything to alter the situation at the moment. He couldn't work worrying about her. And, it would be better if she were close by at this point. If they both had to bug out, it would be easier to hop on a plane together.

"No. You have to come here. Del can put you in a safe house, or I have a good friend you can stay with."

"Sean."

"I can promise you that Ali will make sure you are safe. She was former MI-6. We need to go over everything. We're missing something. I don't want you getting snatched up again. I don't know how long it would take me to find you."

She sighed. "Okay."

She handed the phone back to Del. "We'll be leaving here within the hour."

"Thanks again." In the last week Del had done more for him than most people had done in his lifetime. Well, except Randy and Jaime.

"So, you're related?"

"Long story."

"I expect to hear it some time."

"I promise."

Del clicked off the phone without saying goodbye…again. Sean chuckled as he turned his off.

"So, what was that about?" Jaime asked.

He glanced over his shoulder to look at her. His heart caught in his throat. Damn, the woman was breathtaking. And not just when she was made up. In fact, he liked her like this. She'd left the makeup off today and had thrown on an old Waikiki t-shirt and a raggedy pair of cut off jeans. She just glowed with happiness, even as she was frowning at him.

"I had to have Del help with something."

She leaned against the doorjamb and crossed her arms. "And that would be?"

He sighed. "I'll explain, but not right now. Del's going to deliver something, and I just can't concentrate until everything is settled."

She didn't look happy about it, but she nodded. He sensed that she was shifting away from him, if not physically, then emotionally. He wanted to let her go. It was easier, but after the last few days...he couldn't do that.

"Hey," he said walking to her. He slipped his hands around her waist. "I promise to explain everything. Just a few more hours, and I'll tell both you and Randy everything."

"Is that a promise?" Randy said.

"Damn SEAL," Jaime said, humor threading her voice. "Doesn't the way he sneaks up like that irritate you?"

He smiled. "Yeah, it does."

"Well?" Randy asked. He wasn't smiling, and Sean knew he was serious.

He walked to Randy and cupped his face. "It's a promise. No more secrets."

Sean brushed his mouth over Randy's, then looked at Jaime. "I need to do some work."

She rolled her eyes. "I've heard that one before."

"No, truly. This is regular threat assessment I am doing for Dillon and Associates. I've been doing side jobs for them for awhile, as long as it doesn't require me to travel."

Randy smiled. "I knew there had to be something you were doing on the side. You have never been one to sit still for long."

"Yeah, and I need to do a little work before Del arrives."

"I think that's code for 'he wants us out of here'," Randy said.

"Okay," Jaime said, even though she did not sound too happy about it.

"Hey, why don't you two go out to the beach. It's not that busy right now, and it's going to be a nice day. I'll let you know when they arrive if they get here before you get back."

Jaime nodded and Randy gave Sean a look that said he would take care of it. Sean watched as Randy drew her away and up the stairs. He didn't lie to them. He did have some work to do, and he decided it would be the one thing that would keep his mind off the issue of Emma.

9

Jaime looked out over the beach, taking note of the number of locals compared to the tourists. This had always been a local beach until the last few years. Now, more and more people had found out about the beauty of Kailua Beach Park, and they flocked to it. Thankfully, it was a slow day so she didn't have to be rude with anyone, because she definitely needed to take out her frustration on something.

With a sigh, she moved her attention to the gentle waves rolling in off the Pacific. She should be enjoying her time. She loved the beach, loved Hawaii in particular, and she relished her downtime. She remembered the first time Sean had brought her to Hawaii. She had fallen for the islands, just as she had fallen for the man. Their job was so stressful that if she didn't take quiet times at the beach, she would have lost it by now. She owed Sean for introducing her to Hawaii—and so many other things.

She glanced at Randy. The afternoon sun danced over his golden hair. There were times when it would be darker, but they had been spending a lot of time in the sun lately. The tan he sported proven that. The red trunks with orange palm trees were new, bought in California the last time they'd been on the mainland. She had been the one who had picked the trunks out. She sighed. The man was perfect, just perfect. Oh, there were a few scars here and there. There was the one on the arm where he got hit on his first assignment with Sean. And she knew there was one on the back of his right calf from a knife wound. He had gotten that in one particularly bad situation in Jakarta a year ago. He was like Sean. Each one of those scars just made them both sexier.

She looked back out over the rolling waves. The scent of the salty ocean air and coconut oil filled the air. Usually, it relaxed her. Right now, it was making her fucking mental. She knew without a doubt that Sean wasn't screwing them around now, but she was getting bloody tired of waiting on the answers.

Randy rubbed some sunscreen onto her back. "So, what do you think that was all about? I don't think he was burned, but something definitely went down."

She shrugged, pulling her legs up and wrapping her arms around them. That was what was irritating her. For years, she had been able to understand Sean. Even after their breakup, she could usually tell what he was thinking. It was because she knew where he came from, what he wanted to do with his life. Now, though, it was like dealing with a completely different person. He was a distant stranger; and worse, she worried about his motives.

"No comment?" he asked.

"I don't know what to think."

"Yeah," Randy said as he poured some sunscreen on his chest and rubbed it in. "He's playing this very close to his chest."

"That's nothing new."

He closed the container and tossed the bottle on the sand beside him. "No, but this is another whole level from him. He's acting like he has something else to protect. And we both know that even with our past problems, he has never hidden this much from us. The fact that he won't talk to us is kind of worrisome."

"Maybe not something else…maybe it's *someone* else."

Randy gave her a sharp look. "You think there is another lover in the mix?"

That was the thought that was gnawing at her gut. Sean had always been very protective of women, even if they could handle their own fights. Jaime always thought it had something to do with the way his mother had been abused in real life. She could hold her own in any fight, and he would let her. But there was always a point for him where he would step in. This felt like that and it was breaking her heart.

"Jaime?" His voice was gentle, and she knew then Randy was truly worried about her. Hell, she was worried about all three of them.

"I'm not sure what it is, but I do know he isn't being truthful with us."

He laid back on his towel and didn't say anything for a few moments. "I think you're being a little harsh because you're a control freak—at least out of the bedroom."

She slanted him a look and saw the cocky little smile. Damn, both of them were bad about knowing they had her pegged. It was hard to deny it because they were right. All they had to do was give her one of those looks, or say something particularly dirty, and she melted into a puddle of lust. There was part of her who wished that wasn't the way of it, but that was just the way it was.

"You haven't heard back from anyone about your father, have you?"

She fought the anger that was pounding through her blood. She was still pissed Royce hadn't contacted her about this, and somehow got Sean tangled up in the mess. "Don't use the term *father* for Royce. I refuse to let a man who was never around during my childhood wear the name."

"Did he ever explain?"

She nodded. "He tried to say he didn't know, but I don't believe him."

He said nothing to that. She waited, but he was suspiciously quiet.

She pulled her sunglasses down the bridge of her nose and looked at him. He had his eyes closed.

"What? You don't trust him any more than I do."

He sighed and opened his eyes. "But we both work for him."

"Not anymore."

"When did that happen?"

She shrugged again. "Mainly knowing the wanker got Sean mixed up in this mess got him kicked off the list of people I'll work with. Also, I don't think Sean will be working for him any more after this. You know he was the only reason we were taking jobs."

He frowned.

"What?" she asked when he said nothing.

"Jaime, he's your father."

Anger made her voice lash out. "I told you not to use that term."

"You're blood related at least."

"It doesn't mean I have to work with him. Right now, I don't even want to talk to him, other than to tell him to bugger off for this mess."

When Randy didn't pile on to her irritation, she looked at him. He had closed his eyes and seemed to be enjoying the sun. But she knew better. Randy was trying to avoid an argument.

"What?"

He sighed and opened his eyes again. Then he cursed and put his sunglasses on. "How do all these people deal with this much sun?"

"Not everyone wants to live in rainy Forks, Washington. And quit trying to avoid telling me what you were thinking."

"Okay. It's just that as long as I have known Sean, I have found it difficult to get him to do what I want him to do."

"What do you mean by that?"

"I mean that if he didn't want to help your fa—sorry Lassiter, then he wouldn't have."

"That's what I mean. There is something else driving him—something he isn't telling either of us about."

"That wasn't my point."

"What was your point again?"

"That you can't blame Lassiter for what Sean agreed to do."

She frowned and looked out at the ocean again. She knew he was right, but it didn't mean she couldn't still be furious at Royce about it. Royce had made sure they didn't know about it, so he had done the job without telling Randy and Jaime. It had put Sean in danger, and that was just not something she could deal with.

"He didn't have to go to Sean."

"Yes, that's something I have to agree with."

"Wait," she said, giving him a nasty smile, "I need to record this so I can play it back to you when you belittle my opinion."

"I don't belittle your opinion. I disagree with you from time to time, and that is not the issue at hand. Stop trying to start a fight with me."

"I am not trying to start a fight with you."

But they both knew she was. It was the one defense mechanism she used with both Sean and Randy. She should have realized years ago that is why they were both so important to her on that same level. Everything about them drew her, but in different ways. Randy was a talker, a man who liked to talk himself out of a situation—or snap an adversary's neck if that didn't work. Sean was the thinker. The planner. The man who would have the perfect plan for any situation—with a backup plan that usually had the same result as Randy's. And damn, they both knew just how to get her insanely hot.

"Jaime?"

She shook her head trying to bring her mind back to the present discussion. "Sorry."

"No worries, as Sean always says. But if you were thinking what I think you were thinking, you *must* tell me everything in vivid detail." He wiggled his eyebrows.

She couldn't help but laugh. This is why she had been drawn to Randy. He could always make her smile, no matter what situation they were in. Even in the worst situation, he would coax a chuckle out of her.

"Then tell me what you were talking about."

She thought through their conversation. "You said there was something or someone else this was about. More than likely, it has to do with family or what he calls his *Ohana*, these people he knows here."

Randy nodded. "That's true. It's not like we're the only ones in the business he knows. And, he has that ranch his uncle used to own, the one over on the Big Island. Something might be up with that."

"Cowboys in danger?"

He flashed her a smile. "Eli St. John owns the ranch now."

The name sounded familiar and then it clicked. Tall, built, blond hair. He was a Dom with a lethal smile and a taste for all kinds of women—until recently. She'd heard he had gotten married. "Oh, yeah, I remember him. Former Special Forces for the Aussie Army."

He nodded. "I know that he is very close to Eli and his new wife. He's related to her in some kind of way. Of course, there is always Ali."

She grunted at the name. She didn't really know the woman, but Jaime did not like her. Or rather, she knew Ali didn't like her, so she thought it fair to reciprocate. Of course, turning down Sean's marriage proposal probably gave Ali some justification.

"I don't think we will need her help."

Randy chuckled. "No, but she does have issues, and Sean was like a brother to her. Granted, her husband can take care of anything that comes up, and so can Micah—"

"Micah as in Rough 'n Ready?"

"Yeah. He's Ali's brother-in-law. She's married to his wife's brother."

All the connections were starting to make her head spin. "Hmm, the world is indeed small."

"I agree. There is something else going on, something else driving him. At the moment, pressing him for more answers isn't going to help, but he's promised them. So, why not just enjoy our life right now. We're staying at a million dollar home on one of the best beaches in the world. We are having amazing sex, and pretty soon, Sean will tell us everything."

She knew he was right and nodded. But even as she lay beside him enjoying the heat of the sun on her skin, Jaime knew something bad was right around the corner. One of the things that had kept her alive more than once during her life was her sixth sense. When trouble was approaching, she knew before anyone else did. But, for the moment, Jaime would let things slide. She made herself one promise right then, though.

Blood or no blood, she would kill Royce if anything happened to Sean.

10

Sean paced the kitchen, his office, and around the pool. He couldn't seem to sit still. He wondered if this was what it was like for parents? Other than his mother, he had never had any close relatives, but now all he could think about was what could go wrong. Waiting on the plane to return was one of the most frightening experiences in his life.

"Would you quit milling around?" Jaime said.

He stopped and looked at her. From the way her eyes were narrowed, Sean could tell she was irritated. "What?"

"You're driving me bloody mental. All this walking around, here and there, mumbling under your breath."

He opened his mouth to respond, but he heard the beep from the intercom at the gate. He strode to the box.

"Yeah."

"It's me."

No need for him to say it was Del. There was no way to mistake the growl from the intercom. He buzzed him in.

"Well, he's rude," Jaime said, walking up behind him and crossing her arms beneath her breasts.

Sean shrugged, happy that she was now irritated with someone else for a change. "That's Del."

The moment he heard the car roll to a stop out front, Sean bolted to the door. He opened it just as Emma jumped out of the car. She ran to him as he opened his arms. She came to him easily, as if they had known each other their entire lives. Of course, in the world, they only had each other. Two people who could have walked past each other on the street a year ago and not known they were related. Now, they couldn't even think of breaking contact.

He pulled her back from him and looked at her. She had let her hair grow a bit in the last couple of months, and she had lost a few pounds. Of course, she was wearing her normal uniform for Hawaii. Board shorts and an old t-shirt. She had *slippahs* on.

"Uh, so, do you want to explain things?" Jaime said from behind him. There was a thread of jealousy in her tone. He kissed the top of Emma's head, and they turned to face Randy and Jaime.

"Let's get inside first."

"Hey, Taylor, you want to help with your crap?"

She glanced over her shoulder at Del. "No."

With that retort, she stepped past both Jaime and Randy into the house as if she owned it. Which, of course, she did; but no one else there probably suspected that. Randy and Jaime watched her walk away and turned back to him.

He smiled and just shook his head as he walked to the car. Del was a mess. With his nose swollen, Sean could guess just how bad it was when Del had first shown up. "Sorry about that. You must have picked up on Emma's issues with understanding social cues."

"Oh, so that's why she gave me a concussion?"

"Now you're like family—which means you deserve to know what is going on. Come on, you should hear the whole story because we need advice."

"I think by the end of this, you're going to owe me beyond anything you can afford."

"For Emma, I would sign over the house right now if it meant her safety."

Del gave him a strange look, but said nothing else as he followed him into the house. He introduced him to Jaime and Randy, then walked into the kitchen. They found Emma sitting on the kitchen counter. He had remembered the first time they had walked through the house. She had hopped up on the counter and sat cross-legged on the counter just like she was now.

"Tell me, is there a reason I had to come over here?"

Her tone was what most would call bitchy—but he knew better. He couldn't fault her. She had been through a lot in the last six months—hell, for the last ten years since her parents died. Add in the fact that she was tired and out of sorts due to the situation, she had every right to snap at him. Still, they had to explain just what was going on because they both needed help.

"Jaime Alexander and Randy Young, this is my sister, Emma Taylor."

Jaime blinked, then looked at Emma. Comprehension filled her gaze as she looked back and forth between them. "Oh, yeah, now I see it."

"Half-sister, really," Emma said with a smile.

"Yes, half-sister. And she's the reason I was burned."

Emma shook her head. "You really weren't burned."

"Listen, while I appreciate all of this, I don't see why I need to be here."

Everyone turned to Del. The man was beyond grumpy now, and it was hard to hide a smile at his friend's appearance. His nose was swollen, and his eyes had been bruised in the hit Emma had given him. He was not going to be happy when he had to explain it to his team.

"I don't understand either," Randy said with a chuckle.

Emma rolled her eyes. "You need to be here because you're law enforcement. Sean said you were some kind of team leader, but I'm confused by that."

"Why would you be confused by that, Taylor?" Del asked, his tone downright nasty now.

"You were investigating my house when I got the jump on you."

"Wait, what?" Randy said, as he studied the former Army Ranger. "Is that why your nose is so swollen?"

Del tossed Randy a look that would scare a normal man. "Shut the fuck up."

Randy opened his mouth to argue back, but Sean wasn't in the mood. He gave Randy a look that made his former partner shut up. They didn't have time for crap like this.

"I need you here because I think I have an old friend showing up soon with one intention. I need help with strategy and tracking him."

"Who are you talking about?" Del asked.

"Letov, and he's out for blood—mainly mine."

There was a beat of silence before Jaime said, "Let's have some coffee and get the whole story out."

RANDY WAITED UNTIL EVERYONE WAS SETTLED AT THE DINING TABLE before he pushed for more. The need to demand answers simmered in his blood, but he knew better. It would just set Sean off, and it would waste precious time if Letov were on his way here. There was another factor in all of this. Jaime. She was barely keeping it together. Most people wouldn't see it, but the look Sean had given him as they sat at the table told Randy their lover had seen it too. Her nerves were raw, and her temper was bubbling beneath the surface. One wrong move and someone was going to end up in a body bag.

"Alright, tell us everything," Randy said.

Sean took a sip of coffee before he answered. Nothing had changed, at least not much. Sean hated sharing any secrets.

"I got a call from Lassiter. There was a job, but he called me because of my connection to it."

Sean shared a look with his sister. Randy saw that connection and the shared memory and, *dammit*, he was jealous. Not that it was even sexual, but the fact there was this other person in Sean's life Randy didn't know about until now hurt. Plus, he couldn't get over feeling like a voyeur. It was odd seeing this entirely new side of Sean, and he kept stealing glimpses into the private looks Emma and Sean shared.

"So, Lassiter knew?" Randy asked.

Sean nodded. "Let me back track a bit. I'm going to confuse everyone with the story."

"That's because you don't walk a straight line. You have to do that so everyone knows what is going on," Emma said in a tone that made Randy think she was repeating a lesson she had learned as a child.

He smiled at Emma and his expression softened. They might not have known about each other long, but they cared for each other. Sean rarely let others see what he was feeling, but it was easy to see how he felt about his little sister.

"Okay. So, Lassiter started hearing things out in the field. Things about Letov and his interest in me. I didn't understand it. Not at first, then I realized the connection was back to that first job we did together."

"The FUBAR in the Philippines?"

He nodded. "Remember when we were trying our best to avoid the bastards who were chasing us?"

"Yeah. I got shot, so I sort of remember that," Randy said, not trying to hide his sarcasm.

"The kid who shot you…the one I shot, it was his son. He didn't survive."

Randy shook his head; trying his best to follow that line Emma told Sean to draw. "No, wait, that was MILF."

Emma snorted. Sean tossed her a smile. When he turned back to face Randy, he said, "Emma didn't know what the US acronym was until I told her."

"Let's not get off track," Del said. "MILF-that's one of the terrorist groups in the Philippines?"

Sean nodded and Randy's stomach started to sink. He was starting to get an idea where this was going.

"So, you killed Letov's son? You're lucky he didn't hunt you down and kill you himself."

"True. I take it you know the man?" Sean asked.

Del nodded. "He was selling illegal arms to Syrian rebels. Not that he believed in their cause, but because it would make him money. I also know he was raised by a father who was former KGB. Torture is a family business. Add in the human trafficking and he's a real sweetheart."

"Sounds about right, and I think his son was just getting his feet wet playing a guard. And, yes, they were using MILF to hide. They dressed as them, spread rumors, and it was all about getting back at Lassiter." He looked at Jaime. "Remember going in and bugging his office?"

Jaime nodded.

"He despised Lassiter for it."

"You're saying that your first jobs with each one of us brought you to this point?" Jaime asked; the disbelief was easy to hear in her voice.

Sean nodded. "In order to get at me, Letov started digging. He wanted to know everything about me. He found out that my father was not actually dead. That he just abandoned us."

"Yeah, Dad wasn't all that good of a guy earlier in his life."

Sean sighed. "But, the other issue we found out was that he held onto some patents. And that he had died in 2004. He did have one surviving relative, and she had inherited everything."

Everyone looked at Emma.

"That's you?" Del asked.

"Well, yeah, not that I knew it. I was sort of out of contact with any kind of lawyers. In fact, they were about to file an injunction to declare me dead when I was kidnapped. I had just heard, and I was on my way back to Thailand."

"That's it," Del said interrupting her. "I knew you weren't English."

"Spent the early part of my life there, but most of it in Thailand, Jakarta, all around there." She turned back to everyone else. "I lost my parents when I was fifteen and after that, it was hard to find any kind of records."

"Why is that?" Randy asked.

"I…"

She didn't continue, but looked at Sean. Sean took her hand and gave it a squeeze.

"Emma lost both of her parents in the Boxing Day Tsunami."

There was a long beat of silence. How did you respond to something like that? Hell, he didn't know if he could handle losing his parents *now*, but at the age of fifteen would have devastated him.

"So, when I popped up in Thailand thinking that maybe my dad had left me some of mom's jewelry, pictures…things they kept in a safe deposit box, Letov snatched me. At that point, he put out a call under an assumed name, pulled in Lassiter, who then contacted Sean. He came to get me, and now we are in Hawaii. And thank goodness he takes care of all the other stuff, because I wouldn't know where to start."

"The other stuff?" Randy asked.

"All the money and all that. I really had no idea we were so rich."

"*You* are rich, Emma," Sean said.

"I told you, Dad left it to his kids. You're one. *We* are both rich."

Randy saw the look of disbelief on Sean's face come and go so fast, most people would have missed it. He doubted Sean had ever been accepted so easily by anyone in his life. Randy had to swallow the lump in his throat. Damn, Sean really hadn't had the best road to get to where he was now, but he now had someone in his life who accepted him unconditionally. Randy could see it there in Emma's expression.

"And the burning, it was all a ruse set up by Royce." It was a statement from Jaime, not a question. Every bit of emotion had bled from her voice. She looked a bit shell shocked and Randy understood why. He was feeling a bit shell shocked himself.

Emma studied Jaime, then looked at her brother. "Really? You couldn't tell that she was Lassiter's daughter. She has the same eyes and facial structures."

Sean gave her a smile that Randy would term paternal. "We can't all be as talented as you."

She shrugged. "That's true."

Del snorted then cussed. "Mother fucking nose."

"He has a very bad temper," Emma said. "And uses a lot of bad language."

"I believe you told me to fuck off and called me a wanker not too long ago."

Emma didn't respond, so Sean continued. "Subsequently, Letov found out and kidnapped her. Lassiter got me into Thailand, gave me the layout of the house."

"You really aren't starting at the beginning. Most of this is Letov's making. Way back to when you and Jaime bugged his office all those years ago. He blames you both for everything that happened. That's how she ended up in the hospital when your job with Randy went to pot."

"Wait, I thought we pinned that on someone else. That cult leader in Africa," Jaime said.

"That's what Royce thought, but he was wrong," Emma said. "All the signs pointed to him, but come to find out, it was Letov all along. He lost a lot of business thanks to you bugging him. He had to flee England. Therefore, he blew up the house you were in for a job, then he sent his son after Sean. Only, that backfired. And then, he spent the next five years planning this."

"But, he didn't come after me," Randy said.

Emma looked at him and it was a bit eerie. Her eyes were so similar to Sean's. "He had his revenge on you. You were shot. And, you didn't kill his son. Sean did that. That was far worse than losing business and pretty much being exiled to Croatia. Losing his one child—at least the one he claimed—that was too much. He blamed Sean."

Sean nodded. "Then, he started to dig. He must have been pretty good at it because everyone here thought my father was dead. He followed the trail to Thailand and discovered that my father *was* dead, but he had left a child. He found Emma and kidnapped her."

"And that is how we got here."

"But, wait, if Letov wanted to draw you in with Emma, it seems his plan failed," Randy said. "You didn't even know you had a sister."

"No. And that didn't make sense until Lassiter and I worked it out."

Emma snorted.

Sean smiled. "Okay, Emma really made us work it out. If he had said he held my sister, I wouldn't have believed him. I knew my mother didn't have any other children. I also thought my father died."

"You would have assumed it was a trap," Randy said. "At that point, he had to come up with another plan."

Sean nodded. "Yes. He used one of his identities and hired Lassiter and requested me."

"And that isn't odd?" Del asked.

Emma frowned and opened her mouth, but Sean stopped her.

"Not really. I'm well known in that area of the world; plus, I have connections. He also offered a shit load of money."

"Just like the Philippines," Randy murmured.

Sean nodded.

"I'm still confused. What was the plan if he trapped you? And why didn't he trap you?"

"The plan was for me to watch whatever he had planned for Emma. Knowing his penchant for torture, it would have been bad. To answer the other question, I arrived a day early so he wasn't ready. Or, I should say, his men weren't ready."

"So it failed miserably," Jaime said.

"In a way, but the man is clever and just came up with another plan," Emma said.

"You don't have to make it sound like you admire the man," Sean said.

She shrugged. "Listen, to spend years doing this, he has to be pretty smart."

Del gave her a strange look, but Emma didn't notice.

"Okay, now we have to figure out where he is and if he is coming here," Sean said.

Emma shook her head. "There's no figuring it out, Sean."

"You said that he was smart. Smart people don't let their emotions rule," Del said.

"They do when they have nothing left inside them to continue on. His whole life these last few years were about making Sean pay." She looked at Sean. "Are we going to force his hand, or what?"

Sean gave his sister a sharp look. "What do you have?"

Emma drew in a deep breath and straightened her shoulders. Randy got the idea that she was trying to gird her loins. "He's here. On the island. I picked it up right before Delano showed up."

Cold fear slithered down Randy's spine. *Fuck.*

"No," Emma said. "This is what we wanted. Letov never leaves

Croatia. He hides there for the most part. The fact that he's here means he's restless. He made a mistake coming to Sean's home."

"And he will do something stupid," Sean said. "It's what we have wanted all along."

"Right, then, what's the plan?" Jaime asked.

Randy looked at Sean and understood immediately what he had planned on doing. His heart sank, and he understood why Sean wouldn't discuss the future yet. He had a plan that might make that impossible.

"Now it's time I get used as bait."

11

Jaime's heart seemed to stop beating the moment Sean said those words. Pain reverberated from her chest, and spots appeared before her eyes. The room started to spin as she blinked, trying to control the onslaught of fear that pummeled at her. She realized she was holding her breath. It took tremendous effort on her part, but she finally gulped in air. Randy must have sensed her distress because he trailed his fingers down her spine. Usually, that gave her support, let her know that everything was going to be okay. This time, she knew Randy would side with Sean. And Sean, well, he had lost his bloody fucking mind.

"What the bloody hell are you talking about?"

Sean shared a glance with his sister, which ticked her off even more. This woman wasn't a romantic rival, but they had a connection Jaime could not deny. And she was left out of it. He had kept that bit of information from her—just like he always did. There was part of her that understood why he did it, but her heart didn't want to be reasonable. It wanted to shout and scream. Instead, she curled her fingers into her palms.

"If the bastard is here, the best way to pull him out of hiding is to give him a target. Me."

"It should be easy enough for him to find you," Randy said. "Why wouldn't he just come after you here?"

Sean shrugged. "He might, but I have a feeling that's too easy for him."

"He would never do that. It would be a last resort," Emma said.

Jaime scowled at the younger woman, who just smiled back at her. "Is that a fact?"

If she caught the sarcasm, Emma never let on. "Yes. Letov is seriously insane, but the one thing that has been driving him the last few years was paying Sean back. He will not show his hand if he doesn't have a need to. Using Sean as bait is the best way to get him to do that. He will be watching his every move. Coming here would be dangerous. This is Sean's territory."

"Why do you think that?" Randy asked as he slipped a hand down her spine again. Emma followed the action then looked at Sean. They shared another private look; she turned back to Jaime.

"I think that he would not want to come here. It's Sean home base. Plus, it isn't good for us to sit around. We have been doing that too long. It doesn't bother me, but it is driving Sean into doing stupid things."

There was no doubting from the tone in her voice the barb had been meant for Jaime and Randy.

"So, you just want to go out and hope he abducts you?" Jaime asked, embarrassed that her voice had risen. Way to show how professional she was.

Sean shook his head. "No, that's not the plan at all. I take it that Letov knows my habits, knows I'll end up at Rough 'n Ready. It would take just a couple of nights before he'd pop up."

"Absolutely not."

Sean blinked and confusion filled his gaze. Dammit, he really didn't understand. After everything they had been through, he was just ready to offer himself up on a platter. Worse, he expected her to just go along with it.

"Jaime, I have it under control." He had gentled his tone as if he were talking to someone on the edge about to go over, which she was. She had just gotten him back, and now he expected her to give him up. "We'll go in with mics, and I'll have a GPS tracker on."

Emma took over for her brother, but she didn't even try to soften her voice. "I will take care of all that. We've been thinking the man would show up here for months. Now we can back him in the corner, and we can all go back to our normal lives."

"I will not allow it," Jaime said before she could stop herself.

She could not seem to get her emotions back under control. Everyone stilled and looked at her. Jaime could feel every bit of her control snapping under the pressure. A man who had tried to kill both of them before was hell bent on killing Sean. The idea of dangling him like a big, juicy piece of meat for Letov to come eat was not acceptable.

"Babe, it's the only way to do it," Randy said. He didn't look any happier with the situation than she was, but he was going along with it just like Jaime had thought.

"There has to be a different way," she said. Jaime knew she was grasping at straws, but she didn't give a bloody damn.

Sean went to her and took her hand. "There isn't."

"You could just go into hiding."

Even she could hear the desperation in her voice, but she didn't care. She *was* desperate. Jaime knew she wasn't being rational. She didn't give a bloody damn.

"That won't help the situation."

She yanked her hand away from him, and took a step back. "No."

He looked at Randy and motioned with his head.

"Hey, why don't we go get you something to eat?" Randy asked.

"Because I'm not hungry," Emma said. Jaime turned to say something terribly nasty, but she realized Sean's sister wasn't being an ass. She looked genuinely confused by the suggestion.

"Come on, Taylor," Del said. "Your brother and Jaime need to talk."

She looked at Randy and shook her head. "I never understand why people just don't say what they mean."

Randy tossed them a smile as he followed Del and Emma as they bickered their way into another area of the house.

"Do you want to tell me what this is about?" Sean asked.

She couldn't compose words in her head yet. Right now she just wanted to find a gun and shoot him for being so damned oblivious. Which, she knew made her sound mental, but she didn't give a damn.

"You don't understand why I'm mad?"

He studied her for a second. "I get that you don't want to take a chance on a dangerous situation."

"On a dangerous situation?"

Oh, bloody hell, when had her voice gotten so high and squeaky? She sounded like an outraged fishwife.

"Yeah, but I'm the one in the crosshairs, so you don't have to worry."

She opened her mouth then snapped it shut. His mouth curved, which turned into a chuckle.

"As I live and breathe, Jaime Alexander is speechless."

She shook her head. "Don't joke. Not about this. I can't lose you, Sean. The idea that I almost lost you and had no idea is enough to freeze my blood. I just got you back. *We* just got you back. Now you want to run out there…"

She couldn't continue. Tears burned the backs of her eyes as she looked away.

"Hey, Jaime," he said, his voice gentle and he took her hand again. "Look at me."

She did as he asked, just as the first tear escaped. "I know you think I am some kind of Amazon, but I am not. I can't deal with this."

He wiped her tears away. "You can deal with it. The three of us can accomplish anything."

She shook her head. "Don't play it down."

"You will be there. Del will be on board, and you don't know this about Emma, but she's a genius, truly. IQ and everything to go with it. Her specialty is codes and plans. So, with you and Randy, plus Del and Emma on backup, we can do this."

She tried to yank away from him, but he kept her close and cupped her face with both hands.

"We *have* to do this. I want a life with you and with Randy. We can't do that with this bastard controlling our every thought. If we don't take a stand right now, there will be a shadow over us. We will never be free."

She couldn't fault his reasoning, but she wasn't truly rational at the moment.

"New identities, with new backstory. We could start over."

He shook his head. "I will not hide behind a false name. We deserve to live a free life. You deserve it."

She couldn't help the fresh rush of tears. "Damn."

His mouth curved. "No. I like seeing you like this."

"You like me miserable?"

He shook his head. "No. Human. Touchable."

He leaned down and brushed his mouth over hers.

She sighed and leaned closer to deepen the kiss. He did, slipping his tongue between her lips. When he pulled back, she slowly opened her eyes.

"I love you, Jaime."

She heard a noise behind Sean. He turned and Randy was standing there. Sean gave her one last squeeze before he walked to Randy. Without hesitation, he cupped Randy's face the same way, then kissed him.

When he pulled back, he said, "I love you, too, Randy. But now, we have to get rid of this bastard so we can get on with our lives. We have a lot to work out, things that need to be discusses, but we can't with this hanging over our heads. I need your help." He looked back at Jaime. "Both of you. It could be all done in just a few days, and then we can talk about where we go from here."

Randy glanced back at her. "Jaime?"

She wanted to say no, but she knew no matter what she said, Sean would go ahead with his plan. There was no way to make him change his mind. If Randy and she were there, they could at least keep him safe.

She nodded and walked to them. She kissed first Sean then Randy.

"But, after this, I get a *real* vacation."

∼

"I DIDN'T EXPECT JAIME TO FREAK OUT LIKE THAT," EMMA SAID once they were alone. She had asked to talk to him privately, and Sean had learned to pay attention when she requested something. She didn't do it that often.

"Why do you say that?"

"You talk about her like she's some kind of tough woman."

"She is."

"It's only logical that you are the bait. Letov feels that you are the reason his son is dead."

"He *is* dead because of me."

"One could argue that it is *his* fault. That you ended up killing his son because he was hell bent on revenge. "

"I guess you could."

"Maybe he feels guilty, and he's acting out going after you because he knows at the heart of it, that he had his son killed."

"I thought you didn't believe in analysis."

"I don't. I think it is as plausible as voodoo, but other people do." She shrugged. "I thought it would make you feel better."

He smiled, then it faded. He studied her for a long moment. She'd been spending too much time indoors and her insomnia was back. "What's up? You're not sleeping."

She sighed and walked to the window. "I'm having the dreams again."

He couldn't imagine surviving what she did at the age of fifteen. Saying she lost her parents in a Tsunami just didn't cover what she had been through. "You should talk to someone about them."

She rolled her eyes. "I'm talking about it to you."

"I know you don't believe in therapy."

"Doesn't work."

It was his turn to sigh. "You could get some sleeping pills."

She shook her head. "I've tried them before. The nightmare just continues."

He didn't know what to say about that. So much about her was foreign to him. She wasn't that big. She looked like her mother from the pictures she had shown him. Petite, with short black hair, and those green eyes. Many people made a mistake when they discounted her. But living on the streets for months after the Tsunami had toughened her up. And he regretted that. Fifteen-year-old girls should be plotting fun with their friends, and not wandering the desolate landscape left after the disaster. He wished he could have been there to protect her. Therefore, he did the one thing he knew his mother would have done. He walked to her and slid his arm over her shoulder and stood beside her.

"Del was saying that he has a friend I can stay with."

"He does?"

She nodded. "Cat. Says she works for him."

"Oh, yeah, Cat." He thought of the best sharp shooter of the

Task Force. She was a no nonsense law woman, who would be able to protect anyone. "She would definitely be able to protect you."

"You seem to think I need protecting. I don't understand why."

She seemed so tough, and she was, but he couldn't help the need he felt to protect her. It was stamped into his DNA.

"It's what big brothers do."

She nodded. "We need to end this now."

"Tomorrow night Randy, Jaime, and I will go to Rough 'n Ready, do everything to call attention to me. Letov won't be able to resist."

She nodded. "Make sure they watch your six."

He smiled as he kissed the top of her head. Emma was completely infatuated with NCIS. "I will."

She leaned closer and relished the moment. They had so few of them, and this would be one he remembered forever. They stood there in silence and watched the lights shimmer in the pool. They definitely needed to end it so that all of them could have more moments like this to remember.

12

Jaime watched Emma work on her laptop, still stunned by the turn of events. Sean had always been secretive, but as their relationship had progressed, she thought he had been more open. Now, she knew there were probably other things he had kept hidden from her. The fact that he knew Royce was her father was bad enough. She wondered just how long Sean had kept that little secret.

"Is there a reason you keep staring at me?" Emma asked, not taking her attention away from the screen.

Jaime still wasn't sure how to take Emma. Sean might have been secretive, but he had always been so giving with his affection. Emma seemed to be the direct opposite. "No. I'm just wondering how many other secrets your brother has."

"And your father. I understand being irritated with Sean, but he had no idea until after you dumped him. He had no reason to tell you."

It took a few seconds for Jaime to catch on to the dig. There was no anger in Emma's voice, and she continued to work as if she hadn't just blamed Jaime for hurting Sean.

"I don't believe you should be passing judgment on things you know nothing about."

She shrugged and continued to pound on the keys. "I know he didn't feel comfortable enough about contacting you. That's enough."

"He was trying to protect me."

Emma finally turned to face her. "He doesn't think you can handle it."

That slap hurt more than the last one. "I can handle it."

"You can't have it both ways. He didn't trust you, or he thinks you are a liability. Either way, just know this: If you hurt him again, I will ruin your life."

Jaime snorted, but her smile faded when Emma kept staring at her. "Did you just threaten me?"

Emma didn't hesitate. "Yes."

"I was trained to kill with my bare hands."

The younger woman studied her. "And I not only took out Sean but also Delano. They are bigger."

"You would have to get the jump on me."

"Ah, but see, that's where I got you beat. I might not be as good in a physical confrontation, but I can ruin your life online. I am a world class hacker."

From the way she talked, Jaime was pretty sure Emma was proud of her threat.

"Before you knew what happened, I will have erased your entire life. The one I will give you will force you to hide. No way to travel or earn money. Stranded with a name that will be a weight around your neck. So, just remember that. Oh, and tell Randy he's on the line too. I will not hesitate to ruin you both if you hurt him."

Jaime studied the younger woman and realized that she was being dead honest. She would do anything to protect her brother. It kind of irritated her, but knowing Emma cared so much about Sean was heartwarming. They had both lost so much early in life, and it was good that they could have each other.

"Understood."

"Good."

Emma turned back to her computer and started to work again. She was definitely an odd duck, but she could handle that. Emma was honest and that was something Jaime found priceless.

Sean came back into the room and looked at Emma with a frown. "What are you doing?"

"Checking stuff."

Sean must have been accustomed to answers like that because he took it in stride.

"Del said he's ready to take you to Cat's."

Emma said nothing as she continued to work. Sean looked at Jaime. "So nice to be paid attention to."

The sigh Emma released told Jaime she was irritated with having to explain herself. Jaime was pretty sure Emma rarely had to do that.

"Emma?" Sean asked.

"You said we couldn't find Lassiter. I'm looking for him."

Sean moved closer, as did Jaime.

"You have a bead on him?" Sean asked.

She shook her head and glanced at Jaime.

"Well, don't start being considerate. I wouldn't know how to react," Jaime said, sarcasm dripping from her voice.

"It isn't that I am not considerate. It's that I don't always know how to act in social situations. You, on the other hand, do, and so you are the one being inconsiderate," Emma said.

Jaime blinked. She had just been talked down to by a little slip of a girl. Well, not girl, but a tiny woman.

"Listen, we don't have time for this," Del said. "What do you have, Taylor?"

For some reason, Emma's ruffled feathers seemed to calm. She drew in a deep breath and answered. "It's that there is no activity at all. Nothing on his credit cards or passport. You gave me three names...does he have any more than that?"

Sean looked Jaime. "Do you know of any?"

She shook her head, realizing what Sean had said was definitely possible. Royce was missing.

"Do you have anyone else to contact?" Emma asked.

"No." She cleared her throat, but the knot was still there. "Not really. You know how he works, Sean."

Randy walked in. "What's up?"

"Royce is really missing."

He glanced at Sean. "Yeah?"

"Yeah. Not just off the grid but truly missing," Sean said.

"Now, don't get all mental on me," Emma said. "I said the chances are high that he is missing. But, if I know anything about Royce Lassiter, it's that he is always working the game. Just give me a few hours and I can make sure."

"You need to do it at Cat's though," Del said. Del and Sean shared a look that told her there was a lot more going on.

Emma frowned. "I want to continue working here."

"Too bad, Taylor," Del said.

Emma didn't spare him a glance. She turned to face the computer and started working again. Sean apparently knew how to handle her. He leaned down and whispered in her ear. She paused in what she was doing and closed her eyes. After a few seconds, she seemed to gather herself and opened her eyes.

"Okay."

Del stepped in at that point. Jaime had only just met the man, but she didn't think this was normal behavior for him. He seemed preoccupied with Emma, but then, the woman did break his nose. If Jaime had been in his position, she would keep a keen on Emma.

"Let's go, Taylor."

Emma slanted the man a dirty look. "I don't like that you talk to me like I'm a recruit," she said as she hit a few more keys, then shut the top to her laptop.

Del said nothing to that as he waited, he looked at Sean and nodded. Sean let loose a breath and Jaime realized that during all of this, Sean had had one worry, and that had been Emma.

Jaime didn't exactly know how to feel about that, but she wanted to know more. Once they were alone, Randy and she could make sure they learned the whole story.

∽

It took than less than ten minutes for Sean to get Emma out the door and on her way with Del. He hadn't had enough time with her, and he was already regretting making her go off to hide. It was the best thing for both of them to get her out the door and off with Del. Still, he wanted her there where he could see her.

He sighed as he watched Del's taillights disappear around the curve.

When he turned around, he found Randy and Jaime studying him with identical expressions. "What?"

Randy grinned. "It's kind of cute seeing the way you act around her."

"Yeah. If I didn't know any better, I would say you had the makings of a great father in you," Jaime said.

"Agreed," Randy returned.

He felt his cheeks heat. "Stop."

He walked past them and into the house. They followed him, shutting the door with a definite click. He heard the front door alarm being set. It was already getting late, and they had figured waiting until tomorrow night to go out would be best.

"No, really. You seem to handle her well," Jaime said.

"You sound surprised."

She shrugged. "Not really, but…yeah I am. You are often impatient."

That was nothing short of the truth. He had always had a bad temper. But, Emma had changed him somehow. "I had a few months to learn how to deal with her. I knew she had issues, I just didn't know how much she had been through. Plus, if you think Del looks bad, you should have seen me."

"She wasn't that easy to deal with."

He made his way to the kitchen.

"What was it like?" Randy asked.

"What?"

"With her, when you first found her…what was it like?"

He thought back to that week. The rush to get them both to safety, then the discovery of who she was to him and it was a blow. The constant fear of her being hurt, of trying to figure out if Lassiter had sold them out…it had all taken a toll on him.

"At first, I didn't know who she was. There was something so oddly familiar about her. I didn't know what it was, but her eyes…" he shook his head.

"She has your eyes," Jaime said.

He nodded. "But I didn't make that connection—not at first. Of course, being knocked unconscious might have something to do with it. Damn near felt like I had my brains scrambled."

"Your dad had green eyes?" Randy asked.

"Yeah, I guess. I don't remember him at all, but it is one thing we have in common."

"But other things must have happened," Jaime said, filling the teakettle with water.

"Yeah. She has issues."

"I noticed," Jaime said.

"She's pretty smart, but her social skill set is in need of some work. She was even worse when we first met. It comes from being mainly homeschooled by her parents. She has off-the-chart IQ, but she has issues with people. So, they decided to enroll her in a correspondence school. Her mother was apparently brilliant too. Dad worked all over Southeast Asia, and it made it easier for them to travel."

"What did your dad do?" Jaime asked.

"Something with electronics. A lot of the patents are for things to do with computers. Most of it I don't understand, even after Emma explained it to me."

"I'm still trying to wrap my mind around surviving something like the Tsunami," Randy said.

Sean nodded. "Yes, and that situation just made things worse. Trusting is not something she is good at."

"Color me surprised," Jaime murmured, and Sean smiled.

"Yeah, the first time I met her, she hit me with a two-by-four, handcuffed me, then interrogated me when I finally came to."

"Still, I can't imagine what it must have been like for her after the disaster," Randy said.

Of course he wouldn't, because he had a good relationship with his family. "They were her whole world."

"Then she lost them in the Tsunami," Jaime said with a shiver.

"Yes. I don't know how she did it, but she picked up and went on."

"And she really had no idea she was rich?" Randy asked.

"No. None. Remember, she was only fifteen at the time. I'm sure my father thought he had plenty of time to talk to her. After they died, Thailand was a mess. Remember how long it took to get aid? I don't even want to think about what she went through."

There was a beat of silence and then the kettle blew.

"Anyone want any tea?"

Both Randy and he declined, to which they were labeled as unappreciative Americans. They shared a look as she doctored her drink and sat down next to Randy at the kitchen bar.

"So, you aren't mad at your father?"

He shrugged. "I was in the beginning, but that's a waste. I could be pissed at him forever, but it doesn't let me face him down and ask why. Also, when I got to know Emma, it really didn't matter."

"Yeah, about that? What did you say to her?" Randy asked.

"I reminded her that we would get our vengeance on Letov."

"That's important to her?" Jaime asked.

"Yeah. For Emma, being kidnapped was…well for people who don't have some of her issues it would have been horrible. For her, she almost had a meltdown. When she has them, they are not pretty, and she gets embarrassed. She really wants us to make Letov cry. And she wants video of it."

Randy smiled. "That tells me she really *is* your sister."

"Do you know what will happen when you get this all resolved?" Jaime asked.

Sean shook his head. "Not really. We haven't talked about it. Our focus is getting through this; afterwards, we said we would talk it all out. I'm assuming that she won't want to live on an island after her experience, but she never does quite what I expect her to."

Jaime chuckled. "I can appreciate that."

Sean felt his smile fade. "I'll completely understand if you both want to stand down. This truly isn't your fight."

Randy said nothing, but Jaime's eyes narrowed. "Indeed?"

Damn, another misstep, but he didn't know exactly how to get his point across to them. So, he decided that honesty was the best way.

"Protecting Emma is part of who I am. I love her, although, it wasn't easy to do in the beginning. But, it is my duty to keep her safe. We're family, and the only ones we've got. She got pulled into this mess not by me but because she is related to me."

"And you think we're just going to walk away, leave you here to fight this on your own?"

The moment she said it, his temper ignited. "It's what you're good at."

She looked as if he had hit her. "How dare you say that to me?"

"Listen, I get the whole, let's let things go and forget about the past. But I didn't know what to expect and you can't expect me to trust either of you fully again. You both walked away from me, and you explode back into my life like all is to be forgotten. Well, it's going to take a little time for me to get over that."

She opened her mouth, but Randy stepped in. "He's right, Jaime. Neither of us treated you very fairly."

Jaime turned around to face Randy. "What?"

"Fuck, Jaime, he asked you to marry him and me to move in with him. The moment he did, we both split. If I were in the same spot, I would be leery of both of us."

She sighed as Randy walked to stand in front of Sean. He cupped Sean's face and looked him in the eye. "But know this. We are here to stay. We are not leaving; we will get you through this. If anything, you know that we have your back. We both want more…and I know you do as well. Just get used to the fact that we are here, and we are staying."

Randy didn't wait for Sean to respond. Instead, Randy leaned forward to brush his mouth over Sean's. He deepened the kiss and Sean felt it then. Everything Randy had said, everything that Sean felt, was right there for him, for all of them. Sean wrapped his arms around Randy and deepened the kiss. They pulled back and both of them looked at Jaime. She hesitated until Sean held his hand out to her. She came willingly and he pulled her close, kissing her.

"Okay, you're both here to stay," he said, his heart warming. He hadn't wanted them to go, but he had to give them that choice.

"So…" Randy said as he nibbled on Sean's ear. "Whatever will we do with ourselves?"

"I am sure we will come up with a few things to occupy our time," Sean said.

13

Del pulled onto Cat's street and glanced over at his companion. Emma hadn't said much since they'd left Sean's house. She wasn't always talkative, but she was definitely in shut down mode. That could only spell trouble.

"You'll like Cat."

She didn't respond. If anything, she looked like she had shifted away from him. She was definitely shutting down.

"She's very good at her job."

"Why would that have anything to do with liking her?" she asked, her voice very matter of fact, but Del heard the tension beneath it. He was good at reading people. It was one of the things that made him good at his job and good at managing his team.

"That's not why you would like her. I was just trying to make conversation."

She turned and looked at him. "Why?"

"Why would you like her?"

She released one of her irritated sighs. "No, why would you try and make conversation with me?"

"I thought it would put you at ease."

Emma shook her head. "It's clear you don't like me."

That surprised him and he didn't try to hide it. "I didn't say I didn't like you."

She snorted and looked out the window again. "If you cuss as much at your friends like you did to me, I would hate to see what your enemies would deal with."

"First of all, I'm a guy. A lot of us cuss. I know Sean has a pretty bad vocabulary. Add in the fact that you hit me with a board and broke my nose, and I think I have every right to cuss."

"We all have the right to say what we want. It doesn't mean you should though. There are limits to honesty. Or that's what people tell me."

He caught on to that last bit like a starving man. Del had always been someone who dealt in information. If he could know everything he wanted to about a situation, he could figure out what to do about it. It had to be the only reason he was so intrigued by Emma Taylor.

"So, people think you are too honest?"

"It's gotten me into trouble before. I don't always understand little cues other people pick up on. I often say things that offend others, even if I don't mean to."

Del digested that bit of information, then pulled to a stop in front of Cat's house. "You sound rude, but you're not trying to be."

She turned her head to study him. Even in the cab of his pickup, he could see her surprise.

"Yes. When I try to explain, I make it worse."

Sighing, she glanced past him to Cat's house. She looked so damned lost that he felt the need to fill in the moment.

"Hey, it will all work out."

She looked at him. "You can't know that. No one knows what will happen from one moment to the other. We can calculate every move we make, and it can all explode in your face. Letov is acting erratically, and that works for us on certain levels. But we can't be sure that he won't just pop off. Life is like that, you know. Sometimes things are going along and everything is just fine. Then, all of the sudden it isn't. Plans don't always work."

He knew she was talking about more than the present situation. There was a tone in her voice he had not heard before. She was almost wooden in the way she talked, as if she expected the worst to happen. Just knowing a bit of her backstory made him realize that most of her life had probably taught her that. Losing her parents, and now everything she had dealt with recently, it made sense.

Maybe it was because she looked so sad, or the fact that he had a couple younger sisters, he broke down. He couldn't force her to do something she didn't want to do. He agreed with Sean though. She needed to be in a separate house than her brother. Which left him with only one alternative.

"Would you feel more comfortable at my place?"

She blinked, then focused on him again. "Your place? As in your house?"

He nodded.

"I could go to a hotel," she said in a hopeful tone.

"Out of the question and you know it," he returned in a stern voice.

She frowned.

"Listen, I have a guest room you can use, and it's closer to headquarters where I plan on stashing you tomorrow night. After tomorrow night, you can go stay wherever you want."

And just like that, her tension seemed to drain from her. "You don't mind if I am up? I tend to drive people crazy when I work through the night."

He shook his head. "I'll have no problem ignoring you."

She offered him a shy smile, and he felt as if had won the lottery. "I would really like that. I don't do well with new people."

"Yeah, tell me about it," he said. "Let me go tell Cat you're staying with me."

She nodded and he slid out of his truck to make his way up to Cat's door. His lieutenant opened it before he could knock. Average in height and small boned, Cat often surprised people with her strength. That along with her amazing sniper skills, black belt in karate, and intelligence made her one of the best team members he had ever worked with.

She'd pulled all her hair up into a braid, and she had no makeup on. She was also in her PJs.

"Where's my house guest, boss?" she asked.

"In the truck," he said, stepping up on her front stoop.

She blinked and looked at him, then she snorted.

"What?"

"Uh, who beat the hell out of you?"

It was then that he realized he had just fully stepped into the light. Damn, as soon as he told her, it would be texted out to the members of the team. He was never going to fucking live this down. Hell, he would be lucky if they kept it within the confides of the team. Knowing Adam, everyone in his family would get the info too.

"Never mind. I just wanted to tell you Emma is going to stay with me."

"I can handle her."

He chuckled. "Not sure anyone can really *handle* Emma."

Her mouth curved. "So that's the way of it?"

The moment he got the meaning of her comment, he wanted to kick himself in the ass. He did not need his team speculating on why he wanted Emma at his house. No, wait. He didn't want her at his house. It was just that he knew she was tense about dealing with a new person after everything she had been through.

"No. Emma has issues with new people and places. She's just more comfortable with me."

The look Cat gave him told Del that she didn't believe him. That made her a good detective, but it wouldn't make his life any easier. There was one thing about Cat though. She was smart enough not to say anything about it.

"Tomorrow night I'm going to be at headquarters…something on the side, and Emma will be there. If you can spare some time on a Saturday night, I would really appreciate it. Adam is working too, but I know we'll need backup."

She nodded. "You got it, boss."

"Thanks. I'll text you the info."

He turned and walked back to the truck. Without looking, he knew Cat was already texting the rest of the team about his injury. Sure enough, his phone beeped signaling a text. He glanced at the message from second in command Adam Lee.

So, I understand there's a woman who can kick your ass and you're taking her home. -Adam

Cat was going to be pulling graveyard shift for the next three months. The woman could never seem to keep her mouth shut. He could trust her with work, but personal things…well; his whole fucking team was bad. They were worse than all the gossiping biddies at his grandmother's retirement home. The next week was going to suck.

He opened the door and hopped into the truck. Del was about to say something to Emma when he realized she had fallen asleep. In the weak streetlight, he could see the smudges beneath her eyes. She had spent more than one night burning the midnight oil; that was for sure. Knowing what little he did about her personality, Del had a feeling that her preoccupation with helping Sean had kept her up. There was a good chance that no matter whenever she was obsessing over something, she would have lots of sleepless nights. The fact that he wanted to know more about her was slightly disturbing. Prickly, obsessed women were not his thing. *Ever*. Still, she intrigued him enough to know that after this was done—and if she stuck around—he would definitely try to get to know her better.

With a sigh, he started up his truck and headed to his condo in Hawaii Kai. It was going to be one damn long day tomorrow.

14

The first thing Sean felt the next morning were hands moving over his body. He had barely opened his eyes to see the first twinkle of sunlight, and he was thrown into morass of lust. Fingers skimmed, palms pressed, tongues and mouths tasted and licked. With a groan, he closed his eyes and arched up off the bed. They continued their assault, teasing him. He opened his eyes and found Randy and Jaime roaming over his body. They were both naked, just as he was. None of them really saw the reason to wear clothes to bed.

Jaime had his cock in her hand, sliding up and down before she took his erection in her mouth. Randy made his way up to Sean's mouth.

"Morning, babe."

"Morning," he said. Randy kissed him, sucking Sean's tongue into his mouth. Over and over, he tugged on Sean's tongue; mimicking the blowjob Jaime was giving him. They continued like that, slow and easy, both of them fucking him with their mouths. Sean shivered as Jaime grazed the very tip of his cock with her teeth. She gave the crown of his penis one last swirling lick before she kissed her way up his body. By the time she reached his mouth, Randy moved away, giving her access to Sean's mouth. As she took over, Randy kissed his way down to Sean's cock.

As a Dom, Sean wasn't accustomed to being taken over. He planned the seduction, took charge, and handled everything. He had never been surprised like this by anyone. He couldn't seem to grasp onto a thought at the moment. In this one moment, they gave him something he had never experienced. He could just lay back and feel.

Randy slipped his hand up to Jaime's head and threaded his fingers through her hair. She smelled of roses and seduction... nothing had been as sweet. Or so he thought, until Randy started to deep throat him. Sean felt the back of Randy's throat and almost came. The man was a fucking demon with that mouth. He knew just how much to push Sean, and Randy loved a cock in his mouth. Next, he added his hand to Sean's shaft, stroking him. Fuck. Sean tore his mouth away from Jaime's.

"Fuck, yeah," were the only words he could come up with.

Freed from the kiss, Jaime took advantage of the opportunity. She rose to her knees, lifted her leg and set it on the other side of his face so she straddled him. Without hesitation, she set her pussy down on his mouth. Taking hold of her ass, he pressed her dripping sex against his mouth. Over and over, he fucked her with is tongue. She moved with him, her moans growing louder and louder with each passing minute. The taste of her danced over his taste buds as he slipped a finger between her cheeks and teased her anus. Just one touch jolted her, then she pressed down harder. She had been wet, but now she was dripping with it.

Randy continued to suck Sean's cock, slipping his hand down to tease Sean's sac. His talented fingers stroked the sensitive skin. Damn, the fucking man was going to drive him fucking insane. Sean was about to lose it, come right then and there, but Randy, being Randy, knew it. He pulled away. Sean tore his mouth away from Jaime's tasty pussy to glare at Randy.

Randy shook his head. "Nope. Not yet."

With a naughty smile, Randy slipped from the bed as Jaime scooted down and straddled Sean's hips. She pressed her wet pussy against his cock. Fuck. She rubbed against him as she slipped a finger into her mouth. Something as simple as that was pushing his arousal to new levels. Randy handed her a condom, which she opened. Jaime slid back, allowing Randy to grasp Sean's shaft. He stroked him a few times before he stopped to hold it for up for Jaime.

She took the condom and settled it on the tip of his cock. Then…she did nothing. Apparently she was waiting for him to look at her. He glanced up. She held his gaze as she slid the condom down his cock. Jaime took her time, teasing his flesh as she went. By the time she reached the bottom, he was shaking. The curve of her mouth told him she knew what she'd done to him. Of course she did. The woman knew every button of his to push.

With a growl, he jackknifed up, and rolled them over the bed. She went with him easily, setting her feet on top of the mattress and widening her legs. He pulled her up by the hips and entered her with a hard, swift thrust.

"Oh, fuck…yes," she moaned as he started to move inside her. The feel of her wet, tight pussy clinging to him almost had him, but he controlled himself, for the time being. Randy was watching them. Sean turned his head and watched Randy roll on his own condom; he joined them back on the bed. He situated himself behind Sean on the mattress.

With easy, confident movements, he worked his way up Sean's ass. Being inside of Jaime and having Randy inside of him…it was the closest thing to heaven Sean had ever felt. It took him just a few moments to work that gorgeous cock of his into Sean's ass, then, together, they started moving.

Sean bent down to kiss Jaime, then, he dipped lower and took one of her nipples into his mouth. As he did, Randy dug his fingers into Sean's hips. They were fucking so hard, the massive wood headboard slammed against the wall.

"Fuck yeah. Fuck. Fuck," Randy groaned. "God damn, you feel fantastic."

As they moved together, the rhythm increasing with each thrust, he lost track of time and space. He didn't know where one of them started and ended. In that moment, he knew exactly what it meant for the three of them to be together like this. There was no one left out, no one who didn't belong.

Jaime came first. Sean lifted his head from her breasts and watched as she convulsed beneath both men. He felt the vibrations hit his cock first, causing him to tighten his ass.

"Ahhh, yeah. Make her come again. That's fanfuckingtastick."

He did as Randy ordered. "Come on, love. Come again," Sean said. She was shaking her head back and forth as if denying him; but she arched up, her pussy clamping down tight on him again. He had the same reaction as he did last time, pulling a groan from Randy.

"Fuck," was all Randy said as he increased the speed of his thrusts.

Jaime was coming down from her second orgasm as he threw her into her third. A surprised scream tore from her throat as Sean gave himself over to pleasure. It rushed through him, surprising him with the force of it.

"Yeah, like that," Randy said again. He thrust into Sean twice more before he held tight and his own orgasm took over.

They both collapsed at the same time, earning them a groan from Jaime.

"You two are heavy," she said. Randy chuckled and pulled out of Sean, then Sean moved. After they tossed the condoms, they returned to bed. Sean pulled Jaime into his arms, as Randy snuggled in behind Sean.

It wasn't a bad way to start the day.

Royce felt the late morning sun on his face. He tried to open his eyes, but it took a bit of effort. He'd been stitched up from the shot before they left Europe, but he knew he was barely holding on. He was running a fever, but he didn't know if it had to do with the gunshot wound or from the various open sores on his body. He shifted in his seat and tried to move his arms. They were still tied to the arms of the chair. He was wearing the same clothes he had been in when they abducted him, and he smelled like three-week-old rubbish.

Fuck, he was too old for this. But he had to hold on. He had to figure out some way to help Sean.

"Oh, so I see that you are awake," a heavily accented voice said from one of the darkened corners.

"Barely. Barely alive."

"You're lucky."

Royce used all the strength he had to lift his head and look at his captor. The small stature, the bald head, and the stench of a Cuban cigar told him it was Letov.

"Is that a fact?" he asked.

Letov nodded. "Da."

"What is the end game? What do you need me for?"

Letov said nothing for a long moment, and Royce worried that he wouldn't tell him.

"I don't think that it matters, but you are here for my end game. You know it."

Of course he did, and Royce knew that it was partly his fault Sean had been pulled into this insane game.

"I won't help you."

Again, a long pause. Letov walked closer, coming into the light. His face showed the ravages of living a hard life. He was a criminal, but one that had done and seen some of the worst of humanity. His hair was thinning on top, greasy, and he had gained at least five stone from the last time Royce had seen him.

"I think you might. Because I have something to offer you."

He scoffed at that, actually snorted in Letov's face.

Still, he continued to give Royce that evil smile. "Oh, but I do," Letov said pleasantly.

"What in the bloody hell would you ever have for me?"

He leaned in closer and Royce smelled the whiskey then. It wasn't good whiskey, but it seemed to seep from his pores. His skin had that yellowish tint from cirrhosis. This was a man who lived on the alcoholic beverage. If he didn't get killed by one of his enemies, he was going to drink himself to death soon.

"But I do, Royce. That is, if you think the life of your daughter is anything you would want to protect."

15

Del arrived that afternoon, his grim expression told Randy he wasn't too happy about the situation. It seemed that no one was happy about the situation, but Del's mood had soured since last night.

"How's my sister? She didn't have an issue with Cat, did she?" Sean asked as he showed Del into the office. Del tensed.

"No. She stayed at my place."

Sean stopped in the middle of the hallway. Del ran into him.

"Fuck, Kaheaku."

Sean turned to face Del. Randy had to hold back the laugh. Sean was in complete big brother mode. He settled his hands on his hips and gave Del a mean glare. The task force commander didn't blink.

"You want to run that by me again?" Sean asked, the question seeping out from between his teeth.

Again, Randy was enthralled with seeing the way Sean reacted to news about Emma. It was sweet, and when he got Alpha on another apparent Alpha, well, it was fucking sexy.

Del shook his head. "Your sister didn't want to stay with Cat. She didn't even want to get out of the pickup."

That brought Sean's temper down a bit. "Did she have a meltdown?"

Del shook his head. "No."

"What happened at your place?"

Del blinked. "She slept. In fact, she fell asleep in the pickup, and I had to carry her into my condo. I estimate she slept about fifteen hours."

Sean sighed as he turned and started back on his path to the home office.

"Emma suffers from insomnia. When she crashes, she can sleep like the dead."

"Tell me about it. I thought she would barely weigh anything, but carrying dead weight like that is never easy."

"So, what do you have for us today?"

"Your sister has a GPS device she claims is undetectable."

Sean smiled and Randy saw it there, saw the love and admiration for Emma. Randy was still getting used to the idea that there was this other side to Sean. But, if they were going to be part of Sean's life, then both he and Jaime needed to accept Emma as part of Sean. There was no way Sean was going to let her go, and Randy was happy for it.

"If she says it is, then it is," Sean said.

Del handed him a manila envelope. "There's a burner phone and the tracker in there. She said it should fit on your tooth. Something about how you knew what that was all about. Then she insulted me."

Randy chuckled. "On purpose?"

Del scowled. " Yeah. There are only so many times a guy can get called a Neanderthal before he gets pissed. Like I have never seen a tiny device before."

"Where is she now?" Randy asked.

"At my headquarters downtown, where I'm heading. I've already talked to Micah Ross about the situation." Sean gave Del an irritated look, but the lawman was apparently accustomed to ignoring volatile people. It was one thing that always made for a good leader. "Get pissed and get over it. He has a world-class security system, and he brought in Conner Dillon to work tonight. You wanted backup, I got it. Plus, none of it looks connected to you. No flags because I did all the setting up. No one else in the club knows; and if there's an issue, Micah's telling them they had a problem with employee theft."

Sean nodded, apparently accepting it. "Emma's going to stay there?"

"Yes. I told her she was going to sit her ass there until everything was over and Letov was in custody…or whatever."

Well, that told Randy one thing. Del didn't have an issue if Letov was assassinated. Lord knew the only reason the terrorist had survived all these years was because he had stayed in hiding.

"The headquarters is only ten minutes away from Rough 'n Ready."

"How do you know that?" Randy asked. "Are you a member?"

"First, this is *my* island. I know where big rollers go when they are in town and want a taste of the lifestyle. Secondly, no. Even if I wanted to, with my job, it makes it almost impossible. Add in the fact that I had to pick up Kaheaku's drunk ass the other night so he didn't kill himself or someone else on his way home, so I know where it's at." He looked at Sean. "Micah will keep us attuned to what is going on at Rough 'n Ready. Dillon is making sure we have access to the live video."

"Are we sure this is a good idea? It's a weekend night and should be very busy," Randy said.

"Yeah. Emma has hacked into some of his computers, and there is someone posted there looking for me. We can control this area, so it will be best."

"Well, my job is done now. I get to go find your sister."

"Wait, what? I thought she was at headquarters."

"She is. I am just not sure where in the building she'll be. I left her with Elle in autopsy. Emma seemed very interested in dead people. She's still mad because I wouldn't let her play on our computers."

Sean's lips twitched. "Emma is interested in every damn thing. She has a mind like a sponge. And, she never forgets anything she sees."

Del hesitated before he stepped through the front door. "Her experience with the Tsunami?"

Sean nodded as his smile faded. "She remembers every damn moment. It's why she doesn't sleep well. That and all the energy drinks."

Del nodded. "Stay safe. All three of you."

Then he slipped out the door.

"He's kind of…"

"Abrupt and different, yeah. But that's what they needed for Task Force Hawaii. Plus, when they named him last year, he had no connections on the island."

They wandered out to the pool. Jaime was sitting there watching the beach, but Randy knew her mind was not on the subject in front of her. She still wasn't happy with the situation.

"That seems kind of…well odd."

Sean shook his head. "No, they needed an outsider to take over. At times he has to investigate HPD. Makes it harder if you are related to half of them. Which, you know on this island is about anywhere you go. Everyone is related to everyone else in some way."

Randy nodded as they both watched Jaime.

"She's worried," Sean said.

"That's her job. She worries, you plan, I keep you two from killing each other."

Sean turned and looked at him. "Sounds like we all fit together."

Randy leaned closer and brushed his mouth over Sean's. "We definitely do. And if we had a doubt before, I think we proved that over the last couple of days."

Sean gave him a fleeting smile before it faded. "I guess I need to go talk to her."

Randy shook his head. "Just go sit with her. That's all she needs."

Sean started walking then stopped. "Are you coming?"

"In minute," Randy said. "You go."

Sean nodded and walked over to her. He sat down on the lounger next to hers and said nothing, but he took her hand in his. Randy sighed, happiness filtering through him. The dreams he and Jaime had been talking about for the last few months might just come true. Once tonight was done, they would be able to move on and be happy. And that is all any of them wanted.

THE MOMENT THEY WALKED INTO ROUGH 'N READY, SEAN STARTED having doubts. It was Saturday and it was packed. And the truth was, he had moved away from the lifestyle, finding some pleasure in the act, but he'd distanced himself from playing. Right now, all he cared about was Randy and Jaime, and he knew it would take them awhile to figure out just how they moved on from where they were. Although, they had pretty much worked those things out through the last couple of days.

Micah Ross, one of the owners of the club, wandered over to them. Native American, well over six feet, and what most people would call the ultimate Dom, people moved out of his way as he maneuvered over to them. By the time Micah reached them, Sean could feel heat crawling up his neck. He was starting to remember bits and pieces from his last visit a few nights ago. If Micah wasn't a friend, Sean would probably have been banned from the club.

"Nice to see you're here...and sober."

His humor had a warning edge to it. He glanced over to the

bar and saw Ross' wife Dee was working. "No problems tonight. Promise."

He looked past him to Randy and Jaime. "So, you found him?"

"Yes." Jaime's answer was rude and curt. Damn, the woman was usually one of the best field operatives. The fact that she couldn't seem to keep her tongue in control in public was a bad sign.

One eyebrow rose. "And apparently, you're still working things out."

Sean shook his head. "Kind of crowded tonight."

"Don't worry. Del called, explained that you needed a private table. You get the owner's table tonight."

They followed him. He gave Dee a wave as they walked past the drink area. Since alcohol had been banned about a year ago, Sean must have been lit when he showed up the other night. He was damned lucky he hadn't killed someone on his way over to the club.

He noted a few familiar faces as they followed Micah through the throng. The club had always appealed to him on so many levels, especially the furnishings. It was an expensive club, and it showed as they walked through. When they arrived at the circular booth, Micah leaned down and pulled the table out.

They settled in the booth, Jaime sitting in the middle. He had been back there a few times. The high-backed booths had a great view of the premiere play room. It was the one Micah and Ethan would have occupied on a regular basis, but now that they were married, he knew it didn't happen that often anymore. He scanned the gathering looking for anyone who stood out. Most everyone fit in, but that was the problem. If the person Letov sent for him understood the lifestyle and knew how to dress, they would blend easily.

A sub he knew stopped by the table.

"Evening, Liz," he said with a smile.

The sassy transplant from the East Coast grinned. "Evening. I heard you put on quite a show the other night."

"Yeah." He noticed Randy and Jaime studying the respiratory therapist. While they were both members, they did not come to the club that often. In fact, they rarely spent time in Hawaii. "Liz McChesney, meet my friends Randy Young and Jaime Alexander."

She smiled and her blue eyes twinkled. "Nice to meet both of you." She turned her attention to Sean. "I take it you aren't here to play tonight?"

He shook his head. "No, sorry."

"Well, if you change your mind, I'm over there with some friends." She pointed to a table with several women, who apparently were watching the byplay.

He leaned forward and brushed his lips over her cheek. "You know I will."

She walked off, gaining more than a few glances from some of the Doms.

"She's kind of bold for a sub," Jaime said, watching the woman walk away.

He shouldn't be pleased that she was so jealous, but he couldn't help it. It was nice to know that she still got upset. She had always been a woman who could control the show of her emotions. It was one of the reasons it made Jaime so good at undercover.

"First, she is very good once you get her in the room. The woman has a thing for being spanked by anything from a crop to a cat 'o nines. You know I don't like wimpy subs. Just not my thing."

He leaned closer and looked down at her outfit. He had almost called off the entire operation. The tight black knit haltertop dipped low between her breasts.

"Eyes up here, Sean," she said.

He looked up with what he hoped was an angelic smile.

"Besides. I know one woman who likes to play a little, and she is definitely bold."

Her lips twitched. "Yeah?"

Randy shared a smile with Sean and scooted closer to Jaime. "Yeah, definitely."

The waitress returned with the drink order, and they spent their time watching some of the scenarios. If he hadn't been so on edge about the situation, they would not have lasted long. They did their best to pretend to be interested in the performances for the night, but his gut was telling him there was something very, very wrong. It seemed like something in their plan was off.

"I have to go to the bathroom."

Jaime did not like the idea. It was easy to see from her reaction. She frowned at him and opened her mouth to argue.

Randy leaned closer and she snapped her mouth shut. He tossed him a thankful glance, then headed toward the bathroom. He was stopped three times before he could make it to the hallway that lead to the back.

"Mr. Kaheaku," someone said from behind him. He turned but someone stepped up and zapped him. A force of electricity coursed through his body as he staggered. Pain filtered through him, and every nerve ending in his body felt as if it were on fire.

He blinked as his vision wavered. His attacker was wearing a leather mask, so there was no way he could make out who he was. The man said nothing else, but he held up a phone. There was a video of Lassiter, strapped to a chair, his usually styled hair a mess and his face beaten and bruised. Blood stained his shirt, and he looked like he had lost a few pounds.

"Mr. Lassiter sends his regards."

"Sean, don't listen to them. They only want to get you here to kill you," Lassiter said. "Get Jaime to safety."

It was then Sean realized it was real time and not a video.

For his troubles, Lassiter was given a right hook by whomever held him captive.

"Stop. I'll go."

He stepped forward, but his attacker shook his head. Sean opened his mouth to argue, but he was hit with the stun gun again, and everything went black.

16

Jaime had to fight the urge to follow Sean when he left. Randy had been giving her worried glances, and she didn't blame him. She hadn't been this nervous about anything since she first picked her first pocket. To make matters worse, the crowd seemed to swell with each passing moment. It made sense. It was high tourist season, and it was a weekend. Rough 'n Ready was the only club in Honolulu. They had to be crazy to think this was a good idea.

She took a sip of her water and started to watch the clock. Five minutes since he had disappeared, and she was ready to crawl the walls. Everything was irritating her, including Randy.

"Settle down. He'll be back in a second," he told her as he sipped his water.

"You always just want to let things go."

"Of course, and you and Sean are the planners. Makes things easier."

She opened her mouth to say something, but she saw Micah making his way through the crowd. The look on his face left her blood cold. He was watching the crowd like he was looking for an attack. He was always a man of few words, and he always seemed to be on guard. But tonight, there was something different in the way he looked around the club.

"We have a situation. Come on," he said, not waiting for them to comment. She slid out of the booth and followed him to the back of the club and up to the office. It was hard to keep up with his long strides, and people kept trying to stop them to chat. Randy set his hand in the small of her back and guided her through the crowd.

When they reached the top of the stairs and stepped into the room, she was stunned. She had expected a small room with some monitors. She did not expect all the cool colors or the fabulous sofa. Of course, that probably had more to do with Dee than Micah.

A stern-looking man was there, along with another man, who looked vaguely familiar. They sat in front of several monitors and seemed to be going over footage from the club. If her blood was cold before, it was iced over now.

"Jaime and Randy, meet Conner Dillon and Devon Stryker."

Of course the second man looked familiar. He was one of the richest men in the world, along with being married to the infamous Ali—the woman from Sean's past who did not like Jaime. Both men nodded, but did not look away from their duty.

"Ross, I think they took him out that side door. I told you to get rid of that," Dillon said. She knew of him because their professional world was small. He was also former FBI, and someone she not only respected but also admired.

"It is a fire regulation, Conner," Micah said shaking his head.

"What?" Randy asked.

"They took him," Micah said.

Everything seemed to freeze in that moment, and the air backed up in her lungs.

The burner phone Del gave them went off. Randy answered. "Okay, you have a hit on where they are going?"

He listened as Jaime's heart raced out of control.

"Okay. Send them as you get them. We'll go on your command."

"Clothes are in the back room. You can change here."

"No, we need to stop them."

Randy grabbed her. "No, we need to let him get to where they are taking him. You know Letov isn't here. And you know he had your father. You know that was Sean's plan. We need to follow it, or someone will get hurt. Sean or your father."

She closed her eyes and counted backwards from ten. Then opened them. Randy studied her for a moment longer, kissed her, then released her. "Hurry up. We need to get on our way."

She nodded and went into battle mode, as the men discussed the situation and the direction of the GPS tracker. Jaime knew the only way to get through this was concentrate on the job.

As soon as they had Sean and Royce back, then she could fall apart. Right now, she thought about making Letov cry, and making sure she could take a video for Emma.

∽

They were headed out of the city via Likelike Highway when Emma called.

"Where are you?" she asked over Jaime's phone.

"Put it on speaker," Jaime said. Randy had told her to drive because she was much better at it than he was. He clicked on the speaker.

"Where is he, Emma?" Randy asked.

"It looks like they're headed to Kahuku," Emma said over Jaime's phone.

"Fuck." Randy knew the area, knew it wasn't easy to handle at night. Hell, it was one of the reasons the military trained there from time to time. The terrain was a bitch.

"What?" Jaime asked, not taking her eyes off the road. It

wasn't busy this late at night, but the higher elevations of Likelike got rain, and left the roads slick.

"Lots of jungle. At least, that's the way it looks," Emma said. "And they are already there, which means they flew that way."

"Wait, I think I have it," a voice said.

"Who the bloody hell is that?" Jaime asked, as she sped up to get around a slow moving minivan.

"It's Adam. He works with Del, who has the coordinates too. He's probably about ten minutes behind you."

"What were you saying, Adam?" Randy asked.

"Kahuku has a lot of forest area, but the road they are taking leads to one house. A compound really."

Jaime shook her head. "Only in Hawaii. A compound in the middle of the jungle."

She took an exit, following the directions from the phone.

"You need to wait until Del gets there. He said that several times," Adam said.

"Okay."

Jaime grabbed the phone and cut it off.

"Fuck that."

"Jaime."

"No, do you think now that they have my father *and* Sean in one place that either of them have a chance of living? They don't. Hell, we'll be lucky to get there before they kill Royce. He's served his purpose."

"You don't know that. There are other things going on here that neither of us know about."

"Yes, but if we assess the situation and it looks bad, then we go in. Fuck waiting for anyone else."

Randy was quiet for a second, then he nodded. "Okay."

He knew it might be the worst decision of his life, but he couldn't even comprehend waiting there, holding his dick in the wind while Del made his way over. Letov was known for torture, but more than most people knew about torture. He was a man who had been trained in it. A man who knew how to keep a subject alive just enough to cause them pain. By the time he was done with people, they were happy to die. He couldn't wait for Del or anyone else. It would be them.

"We go in."

He sent up a prayer, then started looking over their weapons. Nothing short of their own deaths would stop them.

~

SEAN WOKE UP, CHOKING ON WATER. HE BLINKED, HIS MIND TRYING to come to terms with where he was. The room was dark, but he could see Letov there, his two henchmen behind him. Then he noticed another figure in the chair beside him. It was Lassiter.

"It's about time you rejoined us, Kaheaku."

Sean tried to move his arm, but found both of them tied behind him. "If you wanted me awake, you should have had your men zap me."

Letov stepped closer, and now Sean had a good look at the man. The last few years had not been kind to him. He had aged at least three years for each one that had passed, and he was bloated. It was easy to see he had been excessively drinking. But his eyes…they told him the most. This man had nothing left to lose.

He knew Jaime and Randy would be there soon, so he just had to hold on until then.

"You always had a smart mouth."

"I don't believe we've ever met."

He didn't look at Lassiter right now. He wasn't even sure if his old boss was still alive. But, if he was, he was just hanging on. Sean needed Letov concentrated on him and not Lassiter.

"No, but I have read your reports. Especially the one where you killed my son."

Of course he had. The man had his greasy fingers into so

many different organizations, it wouldn't have been hard to bribe someone for the report.

"Oh, you mean the one where you sent your son to die so you could fuck with me?"

He knew the hit was coming, but he hadn't expected that it would be so fast and so fucking hard. Letov backhanded him with such power; the chair almost fell over. Sean blinked trying to focus.

"You bastard. You dare say such things about my son?"

He backhanded Sean with his other hand. This one hurt even more. Fucker. Trying to fight the bile that now seemed to be permanently stuck in his throat from spewing forth. He needed to get the man close enough so he could trip him as soon as he had a chance.

"Your son was a fuck up. A big one. Who calls attention to himself when he knows he has his quarry in his sights. Your son did, and that's why he's dead. Of course, you're probably the one who insisted that he go on the mission."

That pushed him over the edge. He punched Sean with such force that his chair did topple over this time. Letov took the time to kick him in the ribs a few times, and the fucker must have had steel-toed boots on. Each time he landed a hit, Sean felt as if he were being torn apart.

Sean didn't move after the assault. At first he couldn't. Pain vibrated through his body. When he had fallen, the wind had been knocked out of him.

"You know they won't miss him for long, sir," one of the other men said. His voice was heavily accented, and Sean remembered it from the club.

"I didn't ask for your opinion."

"Sir, Michael is correct. We should kill them both and just be done with it. It is not safe here."

Sean opened his eyes, and saw the look on Letov's face the

second before he picked up a pistol and shot them both in their heads. Neither man expected it, for they didn't even try to move.

"Thank God. They were getting on my nerves."

He squatted down and grabbed Sean by the hair. "Now, it's time we have a little fun before the end."

When he stood, he grabbed Sean and righted the chair. It took considerable effort, since the man wasn't in that good of shape. Letov then went to his table where he had kept the gun and unrolled a pack. Various sharp instruments caught the dim light from above. But that wasn't what caught Sean's eye. There was what looked to be a bomb on the far end of the table. The fucker had much worse plans than Sean had ever thought.

17

They made it in relatively easily, and that worried Jaime. There was a chance Letov's fast journey had left him unprepared, but Letov was a sick bastard. He could have planned to lure them there to torture Royce and Sean. Killing Randy and Jaime in front of the two of them—before they were killed themselves—would be something Letov would do.

The man really had lived too long. People like him shouldn't be able to cause this much pain.

Randy used hand signals to tell her that he was going to head down the hallway. She nodded and followed his lead. They both had armed themselves with automatics, but they also had pistols and various knifes. There was no way they were not going to get out of there.

They made their way down to the very end of the hallway. All the rooms were empty but the last one. They heard talking, and Jaime knew it was Letov.

The door was partially open, and it was easy to see inside. She could see Letov striding around the room, a sharp instrument in his hand. She saw her father then. His arms were tied to the chair he was sitting in, his face was bloodied, and his shirt had dried blood on it. She didn't know if he was even breathing. Her heart stuttered, as if it were going to stop, when she saw Sean. He was in a chair also, soaking wet, and with a little blood. He was watching Letov as he paced back and forth. Randy made a motion with his hand, and there it was, the almost imperceptible nod. Sean knew they were there. But, he wasn't calling for them to come. Why?

Sean made a motion with his head, and Randy positioned himself to see what Sean was telling him. When he did, Randy's face lost all color. He stepped back then signaled a C and a four.

Fuck. A bomb.

"You would think you would have been smarter. Lassiter said you would never fall for the plan, but you did, didn't you? You just couldn't deal with not flaunting those two disgusting lovers of yours." Letov made a noise. "That slut and the gay boy."

Jaime wanted to go in with guns blazing, but they didn't know about guards.

"Funny you should say that. I mean, you look down on healthy sexual appetites, considering your own."

"What do you mean by that?"

Sean made his own sound of disgust. "It's said you like young girls. The younger the better."

She shared a look with Randy, who shrugged.

"I do not."

"Oh, then maybe it's boys."

"Bastard," Letov screamed as raised his hand and brought the sharp weapon down onto Sean's thigh. He dropped the others he held and backhanded Sean. His chair toppled, but he seemed to be ready for it. The minute he hit the floor, he swung his feet around and tripped Letov. The man went down with a grunt, and she and Randy burst into the room. She kept her back against the wall, taking assessment of the situation. Two of his men were down, shot in the head.

Randy walked over to Letov and kicked him in the face. He

didn't even give the man time to stand. The blow sent him to the ground again, unconscious.

"Get Sean. I'll get your father," Randy said. Randy felt Royce's pulse and sighed. "Strong and steady."

Relief filtered through her, as she helped Sean up, then cut the plastic cuffs with one of the knives Letov had dropped. As soon as he was free, he stood up, then he staggered.

"Hey, there, be careful," she said. "How many more?"

"I don't know. I know about those two, but I had just come to a few minutes ago."

"Royce, buddy, are you in there?" Randy said as he slapped her father's face.

"Take Sean," she said as she went to her father. "Royce, wake up."

He stirred opening his eyes. "Jaime, you're here."

"Yes, and we need to get out of here."

Randy undid Royce's hands and helped him to his feet. "He needs more help than Sean. I've got him."

She nodded and went to Sean. They were almost out the door when she heard something behind her. She looked behind her and saw Letov heading to the table. Without hesitation, she shot him in the shoulder, but not before he hit a button on the bomb. It didn't explode, but she heard the ticking. He'd set it to explode.

Letov fell to the floor.

"Is he dead?" Randy asked.

"Who cares? Let's get out of here before that blows."

They rushed out as fast as they could. It wasn't easy since Royce was a dead weight and Sean was injured. Suddenly, she heard shots from behind them, and knew that Letov was still alive.

"Go," she yelled at Randy. She let go of Sean and pushed him in the back. "Go on, I've got this."

A LITTLE HARMLESS REVENGE

Every bit of Sean's body was throbbing as they cleared the front lanai and rushed out into the yard. Shots rang out behind them as Randy helped Royce. Jaime was right behind them, protecting their back. He tried to turn and see what was happening, but Randy was moving too fast, urging him on. Smoke filled the area as the Task Force Hawaii members were running toward them.

Suddenly, it was as if the heavens had erupted behind them, lighting up the sky. Heat singed his back. He tried to turn around.

"No," Jaime yelled. "Run, Sean. Don't look back."

The last explosion threw them all forward. Randy and Lassiter stumbled, and both of them fell to the ground. Using what energy he had left, he helped Randy up, who then grabbed Lassiter. The four of them made it to the gate, as police vehicles came tearing up the road. Sirens were screaming through the night, cutting into the explosions behind them.

Del was leading the charge as he rushed them.

"We got ya," he said. "We have injured here," Del shouted.

Paramedics came rushing toward them, and Sean finally gave into the pain. He closed his eyes as he was laid out on a gurney. Randy was there, his hand in Sean's.

"Everything is going to be okay."

He nodded, but he couldn't open his eyes.

"Lassiter."

"Not sure, but looks worse than I think it is."

"You should have waited," he said.

"Yeah, well, when have I ever done what was expected?"

He wanted to tell him to stop making light of the situation. Both Jaime and he could have been hurt, and what would have happened then? But, the moment he opened his mouth to say it, Jaime returned.

"You're going to Tripler Army Medical Center."

Jaime leaned down, cupped his face and kissed him. "It's over."

Her voice was filled with relief. Before he could respond, the paramedics returned.

"We need to get him loaded up in the ambulance."

Jaime nodded and stepped back. "We'll be there."

As they lifted him up into the vehicle, Sean looked at Randy and Jaime. They both were covered with mud from their stumble onto the ground. The fact that they were safe was the only thing that kept him from going to find Letov's corpse and setting it on fire.

They would not have been put in this kind of danger if it hadn't been for him. As the attendees slammed the doors shut, he watched Randy and Jaime through the windows, his heart heavy. But how much longer would they be safe if they stayed around him?

18

The rush to get the Tripler ER had left Jaime on edge and had Randy with a headache. When they arrived, Randy wasn't surprised when they were detained. Since the hospital was an actual Army hospital, it was considered federal land. With no clearance or official military ID, they had to wait. Thankfully, as Jaime called the gate guard some rather vulgar names, a massive Scotsman had shown up, flashed his Task Force badge and got them through. They had followed him to the ER, and then guided them to the entrance.

"Name's Graeme, and I bet we'll be able to find Del in here."

As the burst through the doors, the entered a morass of confusion. The small area was filled to capacity with official and unofficial people, not to mention military members and their families. Randy searched the crowd and found Del on the other side of the room near a hallway.

"Have you heard anything?" Randy asked when they reached him.

Jaime walked up beside Randy as Del nodded. "Things look good for both Sean and Royce. Royce will have to stay for a while. He lost some blood, and he's malnourished. Sean has a broken nose and some broken ribs. But he should be able to come home tonight."

Randy released a sigh of relief as the doors burst open again. Emma came rushing forward, a Hawaiian man, who must be part of the Task Force, hard on her heels.

"Where is he?" Emma demanded. The terror Randy saw on her face shot straight to his heart. For all her issues, Emma loved Sean. It was easy to see the sibling worry in her pale skin, and the fact that she looked like she was on the verge of crying. This must be one of the meltdowns that Sean had talked about.

Randy took her by her arms. "He has broken ribs, but he should be okay."

The rather large Hawaiian shook his head. "Sorry, boss, she wouldn't stay put."

Emma tossed a look at her escort. "My brother was injured. What would you do if you were in the same situation?"

Her companion acknowledged it with a nod.

The doctor walked out at that point, searching for someone. When she spotted them, she walked over.

"How's my brother?" Emma asked stepping in front of everyone. He knew she needed Sean, and that he would be able to handle her, but he wasn't here, so Randy stepped in. He settled his hands on her shoulders, and she drew in a deep breath.

"You have to be related to Mr. Kaheaku. He's fine. He has three broken ribs, and he's going to feel like shit tomorrow, but otherwise fine." She looked at Jaime. "Ms. Alexander?" Jaime nodded. "Mr. Lassiter will have to stay at least a day or two. He's a bit dehydrated, and he has a few broken bones we had to set. You can see him in just a bit."

Jaime acknowledged it with a nod, then the doctor left them alone. All of them seemed to sigh with relief. Emma looked at Randy and Jaime. "You two are okay?"

Jaime nodded. "Yes. We got there right at the end."

Randy knew the tone. She was ready for Emma to yell at

A LITTLE HARMLESS REVENGE

her, but instead, Emma stepped closer, hesitated, and wrapped an arm around each one of them. "I am so happy you are all safe. Sean would be lost if something happened to you."

Emma stepped back and blinked a few times. From what Sean had said, his sister wasn't good with emotional gestures, so Randy knew just how much that had taken out of her.

"Why don't we find a place and settle down to wait," he suggested.

"I've got paperwork to do," Del said. "I'll want statements from all of you."

"Tomorrow soon enough?" Randy asked.

"Hell, Monday will work for me," Del said.

"He's dead then?" Emma asked him.

Del nodded, his expression still grim but Randy saw the satisfaction in his eyes. "Yeah, he's dead. Died in the blast."

Emma said nothing as the lawman left them alone.

"Over there," Randy said, pointing to three seats. They made their way over, and Randy realized he now had two women who were going to be worried until they saw Sean and Lassiter. He decided to occupy their time.

"I understand you hit Sean the first time you met him?" Randy asked.

She chuckled and started telling the story of how it had all really happened. Randy just hoped it was a long enough story to occupy their time.

∼

ABOUT A HALF HOUR LATER, JAIME FOLLOWED THE NURSE DOWN the hallway. She wasn't sure what to say to her father, but he had asked for her. After all he had done to help Sean, she at least owed him that much.

When she stepped into the room, her breath caught. He was

even paler than when she had seen him earlier, and he looked ten years older than the last time she saw him.

He must have sensed her presence, because he opened his eyes and looked in her direction. She walked over to him.

"You're alright?" he asked. His voice was so weak she could barely hear it above the monitors. She stepped closer but kept her distance.

"Yes. A few bruises, nothing big."

He swallowed. "And Sean? And Randy?"

"Sean has broken ribs, some other issues, but nothing big. Randy's got a few scrapes here and there."

He nodded. "I didn't have a choice, not at the end. Letov threatened you. He knew about our connection."

"Oh, Royce." And then, she couldn't hold back. The anguish she heard in his voice broke her heart. "It's okay. Everything turned out alright in the end."

"I should have just let him kill me. Sean didn't need to be captured like that."

That thought had her blood running cold. "Royce Lassiter, don't you ever say that again."

He gave her a weak smile. "I promise."

She walked over to the bed and took his hand. "I don't know where we go from here. We have a lot of work to do."

He nodded. "I have a feeling you're going to stay in Hawaii."

"For the time being."

"Then, I guess I need to spend some time in the sun."

She sighed. "I can't promise anything."

His smile faded and his grip tightened on her hand. "A chance is all I ask for."

"Okay. I need to go check on Sean."

"You do that."

"I'll be back tomorrow, probably late, but I will come see you."

"Sounds good."

She hesitated, and then leaned down to brush her lips over his cheek. "I'm so glad you are okay."

He was asleep before she reached the door. She stood there, looking at him, realizing that they both had wasted so much time. She had almost lost him tonight, and until that moment, she hadn't understood how important he was to her.

He was staying Hawaii, at least for a little while. It wasn't perfect, but it was a start.

～

OVER AN HOUR LATER, SEAN SAT IN THE BED WAITING FOR everyone to show up. He wasn't looking forward to it. Tonight was another clusterfuck. It seemed that any time he was involved with Jaime and Randy, he ruined everything. When he realized they had both been in the building…he'd closed his eyes. He would never have been able to live with their deaths. And it would have been *his* fault.

He sat up and grabbed the scrubs shirt they'd given him. He cussed as pain radiated through his body.

"That's not very nice," he heard Randy say from the doorway. With a sigh, Randy walked forward and helped Sean tug the shirt down over his head.

Emma was standing there, her eyes shadowed. "You said the plan was good."

"It was. It just got a little more…violent than I expected."

He held out his arm, and she hurried over to hug him. "I thought I was going to lose you," she whispered. She said it as if she were ashamed of her feelings. He had a lot of work to do there. He knew she wasn't ready to tell him everything, but she needed him. And he needed her.

She pulled back, and Randy leaned down to kiss him. Sean relished the feel of Randy's mouth over his; because he knew it would be one of the last times. When he pulled back, he noticed Jaime was in the room.

"Hey, how's Royce?" Sean asked, knowing that any injuries her father had were his fault as well.

"He's doing well. We...talked. He was more worried that we are all okay."

He nodded.

"I just need my discharge papers then we can go."

She came to him, kissed him, and again, he cherished it. Once they made it back to the house, he was going to have to do something he never wanted to do. But after the events of the last few years, he had no choice.

BY THE TIME THEY GOT BACK TO THE HOUSE, ALL THREE OF THEM were exhausted. Since all of her things were still over at Del's, Emma had said she would get them and return the next day. Jaime hoped the younger woman got some rest, because she looked completely exhausted by the events of the evening. The last forty-eight hours had really worn them all out.

Sean had been quiet on the ride home. She knew he was irritated with the situation, and she knew he was mad. About what, she had no idea. There were so many things to be mad about that evening, but she couldn't deal with that. She was so bloody happy they all survived. As they helped him into bed, she wondered what was going through his head.

"I think it would be best if you both left." His voice held no emotion, and it left her cold.

"Excuse me?" Jaime asked, her heart in her throat, and her whole world coming to a halt.

"This...look what happened. I don't think it is a good idea being around me."

She looked at Randy, who shook his head. It was a warning

not to fight with him. Sean was the worst patient, and could be a real pain in the ass. But this sounded different. This sounded final.

"I think I need a better explanation."

"No," Randy said. "We *both* deserve a better explanation."

Sean looked at them and, in that instant; she saw the longing, the need really, there in the depths of his green eyes. As quickly, it shut down and hardened. This was the stranger she had seen when they first arrived.

"That's it. Just it's best if you both leave?" she asked.

Randy looked at her, and the pain he saw there, the pain that Sean was causing for both of them, was almost too much to bear.

"It isn't a good idea to be around me. Look what has happened in the past."

"You are such a bloody stubborn man. You sit there and say you caused everything bad in life. So, you fucked up. We all fuck up. I have news for you, Sean; you are not bloody fucking God. Get over yourself."

He closed his eyes. "You almost died."

"I have almost died several times. And this time, I wasn't even *close* to being dead. You were. Hell, it is a fucking miracle I survived the streets when I was a kid with my smart mouth."

She heard a suspicious snuffle, and she shot a look at Randy. "You are not helping the situation."

Randy held up his hands in surrender, even if he was smiling.

"You do not get to choose whether or not we love you. You do not get to decide if I can spend my days wondering what would have been if you had not been a coward."

His eyes shot open and then narrowed. "I am not a coward."

"Yeah? Well what do you call this?"

"What do you mean?"

"People dream of finding that *one* person who loves them unconditionally. They pray about it, they join online dating… they do anything to have that special partnership. You have *two* people in your life who love you so fucking much that we went on a suicide mission to save you. And how do you reward us? You tell us to leave. I'm fighting for you here. Randy and I have been fighting for you forever, Sean. But, I'm getting tired of being hurt, again and again. This time…this time, we might never come back. I cannot take it anymore."

"Jaime," Randy said and stepped closer to comfort her.

"No. I want forever. Happy. But if Sean's too much of a coward to take a chance, then go to bloody hell."

And with that, she strode out of the room. She was running by the time she made it downstairs, and didn't stop until she made it to the beach. She collapsed there on the sand and gave into the fear, the anger, the desolation. He would never understand. No matter how many times they saved him, begged him…loved him…he would never accept it. It wasn't until that moment, that she realized it was lost, and they probably never had it anyway.

∽

A DEAFENING QUIET FILLED THE ROOM. SEAN LOOKED AT RANDY, who shrugged.

"I don't know what to tell you, babe. You pushed her too far."

"I didn't do a fucking thing."

Randy cocked his head as he studied him. "You told her to leave. If you haven't noticed yet, that woman loves you. I love you. We want you in our lives. For the first time *ever*, she's thinking it won't happen. She can't keep hanging around hoping that you'll accept the specialness of our situation. I can't do it. It hurts us too much. But I really don't know how we would be together without you. We lose you, we'll probably lose us."

Sean didn't know what to say to that. He hadn't hoped for it, because hoping always ended in pain for him. From the time he was kid, to now…he just didn't know how to handle being happy.

"I can see you trying to work it out there in your head." He rested his weight on his hands and leaned forward to brush his mouth over Sean's, then he pulled away. "We don't need a plan. We don't need anyone to approve. We just all need each other."

For the first time in too many years, hope filtered through him. Could they actually just say the hell with everyone else?

He looked out over the lanai and saw her there out on the beach. She was face down, crying. Jaime Alexander was sobbing her eyes out. A woman who barely ever cried, who did her best to never show emotion, had yelled at him and then ran off to cry.

"She's crying. Not just little tears. That's some serious…damn."

"Of course she is. Her heart is breaking, Sean. Both of our hearts are breaking."

Just hearing that made his own heart turn over. He looked back at Randy. "We've broken it off before."

"This time is for good, Sean. If you don't get your ass down there and beg for forgiveness, you'll lose us both."

He managed to get up and walked to Randy then, irritated, scared, and in so much pain; he didn't know if he could make it. Even with the heavy medication, the pain of his injuries filtered through his body.

"I don't know if I can do this."

"You can."

He didn't want to say what he was feeling. Mainly because he felt like a coward.

It took him a little bit and a lot of effort, but he made his way downstairs and went in search of her. Randy followed him, walking just as gingerly. He found her, kneeling in the sand, her face wet with tears.

It broke his fucking heart.

"Jaime…"

"What?" she spat out. Oh, princess never did like showing her emotions.

"I shouldn't have said it. I was trying to…"

In that moment, she looked up at him, her eyes filled with unshed tears, and he knew he couldn't send her away. He couldn't send either of them away. They were the reason he got out of bed every morning, the only people who would truly understand him. The only two who would love him like he needed to be loved.

He eased his way down onto the sand, knowing he would pay for it when the pain meds wore off. "I'm sorry. I was being an ass. Don't leave." He looked behind him to Randy. "Either of you. I want you to stay, to be with me. "

Jaime shook her head, and his heart sank.

"Are you saying no?"

"Don't ask because you're afraid of being alone."

It was his turn to shake his head, and he instantly regretted it. "Afraid of being alone? Woman, I just told you two to leave. Where do you get such asinine ideas?"

"It's why I said no to your marriage proposal. You freaked me out, and I knew that you were just upset that we might be split up as partners."

"I proposed to you because I love you. Of all the dumbass, insane reactions."

"And, I wasn't ready. Randy and I talked about it. We both freaked out and ran away because, well, you were so sure and we weren't. Different times, but we both had the same reaction. I never—" Randy coughed, and she smiled as she wiped away tears. "Randy and I never thought we would get another chance. But we have it, and I want you. I want you and Randy and say fuck everyone else in our lives. This is what matters."

Joy filled his entire being and made him so dizzy. When he stood up, he realized it might have more to do with the pain drugs. He stumbled, and Randy caught him.

"Whoa, there, babe," Randy said, as he helped Sean stand

upright. When he was face-to-face with him, Randy kissed him. "Everything she said and more."

Jaime stood up, put an arm around each one of them. "Let's go to bed. This has been kind of a sucky week on the injury front."

"Don't worry, princess, we'll both be back in shape to keep you happy soon."

She laughed, and Sean let the sound rush over him. Nothing sounded better than that.

EPILOGUE

*E*mma and Sean sat in silence as they looked out over the ocean. Del had dropped her off an hour earlier, and she had asked to talk to Sean alone. He had consented, as he always did. It was odd to be so comfortable with another human being. At least, it was for her. But, from the moment she and Sean had settled their differences in Thailand, she had been comfortable with him.

"So, you've decided to stay here?" she asked.

He nodded, his expression lighter than she had ever seen it. "Well, sort of. First, I wanted to clear it with you."

"Why?"

"I want to be close to you."

She didn't smile, though she wanted to. It had been so long since another human had worried about her that way. When he had burst into her life six months earlier, she thought she could walk away. She didn't need a half-brother. But, truth was, she did need him.

"Do you think you can earn a living here? I mean, outside of handling my stuff?"

"We can pick up some jobs here and there, but we've been

talking about opening our own firm. But to keep us busy, Conner Dillon is always looking for contractors who don't want to work full time."

"That's good. You need a home."

He glanced at her. "There is plenty of space for you. I bought this with you in mind."

She rolled her eyes. "No thanks."

"You don't want to live with your big brother?" he asked, humor lacing his voice. Still, she heard something else, something close to hurt.

With a sigh, she forced herself to look away from the ocean and give him her full attention. Her brother. They didn't look that much alike, but she saw herself in his eyes, and his high cheekbones. It was hard to imagine that she now had someone else in her world, someone who belonged to her.

"Not really. No offense, but living with another person would be a challenge for me."

Sympathy filled his expression, and she shook her head. She hated the look. That's why she rarely told people her entire story. The pity wasn't for her. It was so they could feel better about themselves.

"No, don't do that. Don't pity me."

"I don't pity you. Why would I? A world class mind, definitely can take care of yourself, but I would like to get to know you better."

"Well, I guess I could stay in Hawaii." She glanced back at the house, then looked at him. "I take it you're all together?"

He nodded. It still seemed odd to her, but what did she know. Other than her parents, she had only had one long-term relationship with another human, and that was Sean. Emma didn't even know how to deal with a relationship with one person, let alone two.

"Too many people."

He chuckled. "Passing judgment?"

"No. I just can't imagine putting up with another person in my personal space all the time. Having two, ugh."

He laughed then, a big belly laugh that echoed over the sweet Hawaiian air. "You do make me happy, Emma."

"Are you really happy? Are they treating you right?"

His expression softened. "Yeah, they are. Looking out for me?"

"You're the only brother I have. And I have ways of making people pay."

"Is that a fact?"

She nodded. "I can get into a person's life, and before they know it, they have nothing left. No job, no money, no house."

"You're kind of scary."

She nodded. "I protect what's mine."

He smiled and chucked her under the chin. "Then, I count myself lucky."

They went back to watching the waves roll in. Considering how she lost her parents, she knew most people would think she would want to stay as far away from the ocean as possible. "I was already thinking about staying here though."

"Oh?"

"Yeah. Delano talked to me about a job. Not full time, but some kind of contract work. They need a person with my skill set."

"I didn't know you were interested in that kind of work."

She shrugged. "Not sure if I am, but solving crimes is like solving puzzles. I like puzzles."

"So, you would stay here. Are you sure?"

She knew what he was asking, but she had returned to Thailand. It had been hard to do, but she had done it. She could handle Hawaii, especially if her family was here.

"Yeah, I can stay. Anywhere I live is going to have some kind of natural disaster. I would much rather deal with a Tsunami warning than a tornado. Those bastards just drop out of the sky."

He chuckled. Suddenly they heard something crash in the kitchen.

"I said to let me get it for you," Randy said, his voice calm and filled with humor.

"Well, if you two would not put important things on the top shelf, I wouldn't have issues. We are not all bloody giants."

"You do have a lot of stuff on the high shelves," Emma said.

"She lives with two men who are over six feet tall. You would think she would ask one of us."

"Sometimes, a woman has to do for herself."

Something clattered to the floor, and this time it sounded as if glass had shattered.

"It's not normal, but it's home," she said.

His chuckled turned into a full-blown laugh, as she leaned her head on his shoulder. They might not be the average *Ohana*, but it was nice to have them around. Maybe, she might have just found her home.

GET DEL AND EMMA'S STORY...

Martin Delano and Emma Taylor's story in the first Task Force Hawaii book, Seductive Reasoning. Get more info on Melissa's website or at the end of this book in the Original Harmless Section.

THANK YOU

Thank you so much for reading A Little Harmless Revenge. If you enjoyed Randy, Sean, and Jaime, please tell friends about the book and if you have the time, I would truly appreciate a review at your favorite online retailer.

Thank,
Mel

A LITTLE HARMLESS SCANDAL

COMING 10-3-17

For the first time two years, a brand new Harmless book!

Preorder the Book

Wanting two men isn't the smart thing to do, but falling for both of them might just ruin all their lives.

Adam Fullerton and **Mick McGrath** have been a couple for over five years but they always knew something was missing. They have brought more than one woman into their bed, but none of them had enticed them into a more permanent relationship. That is, until the meet photographer **Serenity Jones**.

Serenity lives a simple life, one far from her childhood as a star of one of most popular sitcoms on TV. She'd been the poster child for an out of control teen and had more than one deranged fan. She got herself clean, changed her name, and disappeared. She avoids anything that might attract the tabloids and that definitely includes the Mick and Adam. Even knowing that, she allows them to tempt her into a night of pleasure.

After that night, none of them are ready to walk away. But soon, Serenity's former life comes back to haunt her as tabloids catch whiff of her new relationship. As the scandal erupts around them, the threesome must learn to stand together, or lose the fragile new relationship.

>>Warning: This book includes two hot bisexual men, one very interested woman, and lots of smexy scenes including all three of them. Also has much Hawaiian scenery, a trip to Rough 'n Ready (and a scene with Micah Ross), along with a scenes so hot, it will melt your e-reader and curl your toes. As any Harmless Addict will tell you, ice water and towels are recommended while reading.

ABOUT THE AUTHOR

From an early age, USA Today Bestselling author Melissa loved to read. First, it was the books her mother read to her including her two favorites, Winnie the Pooh and the Beatrix Potter books. She cut her preteen teeth on Trixie Belden and read and reviewed To Kill a Mockingbird in middle school. It wasn't until she was in college that she tried to write her first stories, which were full of angst and pain, and really not that fun to read or write. After trying several different genres, she found romance in a Linda Howard book.

Since her first published book, Grace Under Pressure, Mel has had over 60 short stories, novellas, and novels published. She has written in genres ranging from historical to contemporary to futuristic and has worked with 8 publishers although she handles most of her publishing herself. She is best known for her Harmless and Santini series.

After years of following her military husband around the country and world, Mel happily lives with her family in horse and wine country in Northern Virginia.

Get more info about Mel:
Facebook: MelissaSchroederfanpage
Twitter: Melschroeder

Instagram: Melschro

Pinterest: MelissaSchro

Join Mel and her fans in her private fan group to get early cover reveals and excerpts.

Facebook.com/groups/harmlesslovers

www.melissaschroeder.net
Melissa@MelissaSchroeder.net

ALSO BY MELISSA SCHROEDER

HARMLESS

A Little Harmless Sex

A Little Harmless Pleasure

A Little Harmless Obsession

A Little Harmless Lie

A Little Harmless Addiction

A Little Harmless Submission

A Little Harmless Fascination

A Little Harmless Fantasy

A Little Harmless Ride

A Little Harmless Secret

A Little Harmless Revenge

THE HARMLESS SHORTS

Max and Anna

Chris And Cynthia

Evan and May

Micah and Dee

A LITTLE HARMLESS MILITARY ROMANCE

Infatuation

Possession

Surrender

THE SANTINIS

Leonardo

Marco

Gianni

Vicente

A Santini Christmas

A Santini in Love

Falling for a Santini

One Night with a Santini

A Santini Takes the Fall

A Santini's Heart

SANTINI BUNDLES
VOLUME ONE
VOLUME TWO

SEMPER FI MARINES

Tease Me

Tempt Me

Touch Me

The Semper Fi Marines Collection

THE FITZPATRICKS

The Lost Night-free prequel

At Last

TASK FORCE HAWAII

Seductive Reasoning

Hostile Desires

Constant Craving

Tangled Passions

Task Force Hawaii Vol 1

TEXAS TEMPTATIONS

Conquering India

Delilah's Downfall-returning soon

ONCE UPON AN ACCIDENT

An Accidental Countess

Lessons in Seduction

The Spy Who Loved Her

THE CURSED CLAN

Callum

Angus

Logan

BY BLOOD

Desire by Blood

Seduction by Blood

BOUNTY HUNTER'S, INC

For Love or Honor

Sinner's Delight

THE SWEET SHOPPE

Cowboy Up

Tempting Prudence

LONESTAR WOLF PACK

The Alpha's Saving Grace

CONNECTED BOOKS

The Hired Hand

Hands on Training

A Calculated Seduction

Going for Eight

SINGLE TITLES

Grace Under Pressure

Telepathic Cravings

Her Mother's Killer

The Last Detail

Operation Love

Chasing Luck

The Seduction of Widow McEwan

Snowbound Seduction

Dallas Fire and Rescue KW: Scorched

COMING SOON

A Little Harmless Scandal

THE ORIGINAL HARMLESS SERIES

Twelve years, eleven books, two spinoffs, a serial…it's all HARMLESS!
All contemporary, books include elements of BDSM, Suspense, Military, and is one of the most diverse series available today!

I

HARMLESS

IT'S ALL HARMLESS UNTIL SOMEONE FALLS IN LOVE.

A LITTLE HARMLESS SEX

BOOK ONE

Is it love, or just a little harmless sex?

READ AN EXCERPT | BUY THE BOOK

Max has always been **Anna**'s knight in shining armor. But Max has always seen her as a charming, and very sexy, little sister. Until Max's cold fiance dumps him, Anna unloads another of her many conquests and she invites him over for margaritas and Mexican food. Too much tequila, too much flirting, and too many years of fighting the attraction — Max loses control and has mind-blowing sex with Anna on her couch. And in her shower. And in her bed. When the sun rises the next morning, both of them must face that their night together is just the first of many.

For Max, he knows he wants Anna forever, but convincing a commitment-phobe like Anna is no easy task. For Anna, she can't believe she has finally slipped beneath Max's steely self-control. He is every woman's dark, wet fantasy come true. But what happens when Max pushes Anna for more than just A Little Harmless Sex?

»**WARNING: The following book contains: explicit sex, graphic terms for body parts, torture via silk stockings, a little spanking, and shower and office sex.**

A LITTLE HARMLESS PLEASURE

BOOK TWO

A night of forbidden pleasures leads to more than either of them expected.
READ AN EXCERPT | BUY THE BOOK

Cynthia Myers meets Chris Dupree at her former fiancé's wedding. After a little dancing, and champagne, she ends up back in Chris's hotel room. For one night of down and dirty sex. That's it, that's all. He lives far away, and she has other things to do… like get a life.

Chris is a switch. He likes to dominate but he also likes to play the role of a submissive from time to time. His last relationship with a sub turned nasty and since then, he has shied away from anything but straight vanilla sex. When he meets Cynthia, he finds a woman who could change his mind. His mate. The only problem is he has to convince her.

In a carefully orchestrated seduction, Chris teaches Cynthia about submission and dominance, allowing her to take the reins. As he leads her through pleasures she thought she'd never experience, Cynthia's self confidence soars and she finds herself falling in love with him. But, when he asks for submission in the bedroom, can she surrender to prove her love or was it all about a little harmless pleasure?

» WARNING: The following book contains: Lots of sex, of course; bondage and submission done in a tasteful but wonderfully arousing way, propositions from a drunken woman, hot phone sex, southern accents, Hawaiian scenery, and OH MY, a m/f/m ménage that will send tingles all the way to your toes, along with other various body parts. A glass of ice-cold water for refreshment is recommended while reading.

A LITTLE HARMLESS OBSESSION

BOOK THREE

What begins as a quest for submission becomes an unrelenting need for love.
READ AN EXCERPT | BUY THE BOOK

May **Aiona**'s crush on sexy **Evan Chambers** is a bad habit that should be easy to break. It's not like he's ever noticed her. Looking for a safe place to release the reins of control and explore her curiosity about BDSM, May takes a friend up on an invitation to visit an exclusive bondage club—all she has to agree to is a public submission.

Evan can't help but notice the exotically beautiful May. But despite his success, the dirty secrets of his past whisper that he'll never be good enough for her. When Evan sees her standing in his club ready to submit to his best friend, he gives in to the thing he wants most—May as his sub. After their session, he knows one night will never be enough. But loving May isn't easy for a man always ready to take charge. She might like to submit in the bedroom, but she doesn't like anyone telling her what to do outside of it.

When May insists she's not in any danger from the person

seemingly obsessed with her, she ends up in the sights of a deranged stalker—with Evan possibly too far away to help.

» WARNING: The following book contains: sexy Hawaiian settings, crazy relatives, and a submission scene that leaves the heroine breathless and the hero frustrated. There are toys, bondage, and love scenes so hot, you'll need ice water and a towel. Remember, it's a Harmless story, so you know there's nothing harmless about it.

A LITTLE HARMLESS LIE

BOOK FOUR

Falling for her might be easy, seducing her may be damned hard, but keeping her alive might just be deadly.

READ AN EXCERPT | BUY THE BOOK

Coming from nothing, **Micah Ross** now has more than he knows what to do with. His Hawai'i BDSM club is flourishing, and he has his pick of women. Except one. **Dee Sumners** is cute, sexy, feisty…and, since she's on his payroll, off-limits. Plus, she insists she isn't into the life. Until one heated kiss hints that his head bartender secretly hungers to be his sub.

Life on the run doesn't allow Dee to indulge in long-term relationships. Still, Micah manages to work his way through her tough armor and under her skin. Yet even as she succumbs to his skilled seduction, her survival instinct forms a plan to leave the island she has grown to love—and the man she's in danger of loving.

When Dee disappears, Micah's anger turns to fear when he realizes she didn't leave willingly. Calling on his skills as a former bounty hunter, he tracks her to the mainland only to discover she is entangled in a web of lies and deceit that not only threatens their love, but her life.

» **WARNING: The following book contains: more Hawaiian settings, a Native American Dom who always thinks he's right, a woman on the run, sexy kisses, murderous relatives, a trip to Sin City, and a seduction that is sweet and hot and everything in between. Ice water and a towel are recommended while reading.**

A LITTLE HARMLESS ADDICTION

BOOK FIVE

Falling in love might not be the smart thing, but it might be the one thing they both need.

READ AN EXCERPT | BUY THE BOOK

*J*ocelyn Dupree has come to Hawaii to heal. After a horrific experience with her last boss, she is on the mend and ready to start again. She is focused on rebuilding her life and her career as a pastry chef. She definitely doesn't need a man in her life, or so she thinks.

Kai Aiona has always been the guy to mend a broken heart. Unfortunately, the last heart that was broken was his. He has sworn off damaged women, but he can't resist Jocelyn's sad eyes, not to mention her determination to succeed.

One little date turns into several and soon, Jocelyn finds herself easily addicted to Kai's sensual nature. Resisting him becomes impossible, but Jocelyn isn't ready to trust completely. When Kai discovers she hasn't been telling him everything, Jocelyn is left with two choices: trust her heart, or let the one man she has ever loved go.

»WARNING: The following book the following: Scenes from Hawaii, nosey friends and family, two people who are right for each other but too stupid to realize it, a tattooed and pierced hero, a sassy Southern heroine, one drunken night, and love scenes that will curl your toes, warm your heart and leave you panting for more. Remember, Harmless stories are not for the weak.

A LITTLE HARMLESS SUBMISSION

BOOK SIX

For a tough-as-nails Dom, hunting a sadistic serial killer is nothing compared to losing his heart.

READ AN EXCERPT | BUY THE BOOK

Rome Carino is hunting a predator. One who likes to hurt submissives and the most popular BDSM club's patrons are being targeted. With each fresh kill, he gets more brazen. Rome knows he just needs one little break, but before he can make headway, the FBI shows up. Worse, the uptight, buttoned-down Special Agent **Maria Callahan** suggests a plan that is dangerous, but worth it because it might just catch the killer. If Rome can keep his mind on the case and off the beautiful FBI agent, he'll be just fine.

Maria is still trying to step out of her legendary father's shadow and knows just how to do it. Luring the killer by posing as Rome's new sub seems like a good idea. That is, until undercover becomes real life and she finds herself tangled up with a man who amazes and scares her at the same time. Her growing attraction to the Honolulu Police Detective is a little too much to handle. Even knowing that, she can't help falling in love with the tough Dom and losing herself in the games they play in the bedroom.

Rome is overwhelmed by his need for Maria. He has never had a sub respond to him the way she does and no matter what he does, he feels himself slipping off that cliff into love. As their relationship starts to unfold, he realizes that he will do anything to win her heart, to convince her to become his sub for a lifetime. But before he can do anything, the killer turns his attention on Rome and the one thing he holds dear: Maria.

» **WARNING: The following book contains: A Dom who thinks he can do no wrong, a new sub who is about to teach him he can, palm trees, a trip or two to Rough 'n Ready, a flirty Aussie Dom with questionable motives, old friends, and a new enemy. Yeah, it might be called Harmless, but you Addicts know it's anything but.**

This book is reissue and has not been substantially changed.

A LITTLE HARMLESS FASCINATION

BOOK SEVEN

Wanting her isn't smart, seducing her is inevitable, but falling in love with her could be downright deadly for both of them.

READ AN EXCERPT | BUY THE BOOK

Security expert **Conner Dillon** isn't a man who often takes a vacation. So when he is ordered to take a month off, and his sister insists on a trip to Hawaii, he isn't very happy. But, after seeing his landlady **Jillian Sawyer** again, he might just find something — or someone — to occupy his time.

For years, Jillian has always had a crush on Conner. Now an erotic romance author with a thing for Doms, she finds herself beyond intrigued by the man. He is good to the core, but there is something else darker in him that calls to her.

After one night in bed, they both find themselves addicted. In Jillian, Conner has found the perfect sub…and in him she finds someone she can trust. Falling in love isn't what they expected, but walking away is impossible—especially when they realize someone wants Jillian dead.

»**WARNING: The following book contains: An uptight**

security expert who prefers schedules, a romance writer who does not, tattoos, a trip to the Aloha Swap Meet, two hunky neighbors who irritate our hero, and of course this would not be a Harmless book without a trip to Rough 'n Ready. Ice is recommended as any Harmless Addict will tell you, but the author takes no responsibility if a reader should become overheated. Read at your own risk.

This book is a reissue and has not been substantially changed.

A LITTLE HARMLESS FANTASY

BOOK EIGHT

What starts out as simple fantasy among friends, becomes an overwhelming need that none of them can deny.

READ AN EXCERPT | BUY THE BOOK

Maura Dillon has always been someone who lived life on her own terms. From the time she in college she knew she had different needs than most of her friends. But she never thought she would find herself torn between two very sexy men, or that they would want to add her to their relationship.

Zeke and **Rory** have known each other for years. Their casual relationship has spanned a decade, but now that they are living together things are on a whole other level. Add in their mutual attraction for Maura and things are just getting out of hand.

Rory understands their desires and suggests a week in Hawaii. No rules, no limits, no regrets. But as their nights are filled with unimaginable erotic pleasure, there is someone lurking in the shadows. Someone who wants revenge, and will stop at nothing to succeed.

»WARNING: this book contains the following: Two sexy men who are hot for each other and the heroine, more Hawaiian scenery, a Dom who thinks he can control everything, two lovers who know he can't, and scenes that push even Harmless Addicts over the edge.

This book is a reissue and has not been substantially changed.

A LITTLE HARMLESS RIDE

BOOK NINE

When this Dom falls hard, he will do anything to protect the woman he loves.

READ AN EXCERPT | BUY THE BOOK

Elias St John has lived a life most people wouldn't believe. An Aussie by birth, he has found his way to the Big Island working as the right hand man to Joe Kaheaku. When his boss dies and leaves the ranch to Eli and Joe's niece **Crysta Miller**, Eli finds himself more than a little attracted to her.

After finding her fiancé in bed with another woman and helping her father through his illness, Crysta is ready for a new start. The offer of the ranch far away from home is perfect. The only problem she has is with Eli who constantly tells her what to do. When an argument turns into a passionate kiss, both of them get more than they were expecting.

Eli finds himself completely enthralled with Crysta as his submissive. As seemingly simple accidents turn deadly, Eli realizes that someone is bent on destroying the ranch by any means possible—even murder.

» WARNING: this book contains the following: A cynical Dom, a woman ready for adventure, Hawaiian cowboys-yeah they have them, horse rides, stunning sunsets and a new island for Addicts to cherish. Remember, it's Harmless so bring on the ice water and towels.

A LITTLE HARMLESS SECRET

BOOK TEN

Just because you love someone doesn't mean you can trust them.

READ AN EXCERPT | BUY THE BOOK

Devon Stryker is a man with no past—not one anyone can dig up that is. His made up identity has kept him safe from everyone, except one woman. Five years earlier he let his guard down once, one night of unforgettable passion. He has yet to get her out of his mind. When he thinks he sees her in Seattle, he becomes obsessed with finding her.

Alicia Hughes hasn't forgotten Devon either. She had been on assignment from MI-6 to find him. Since he disappeared, her life has fallen apart. When she comes face to face with the one man she loved—and the one she fears the most—she panics. When he catches up to her, he finds the woman he has always loved—and the child they made together.

As the old lovers form a tentative alliance, the feelings they both had for each other rise to the surface. They have to let those things go to protect everything they hold dear in the world because someone is intent on destroying them…by any means possible.

»**WARNING: This title includes secrets, guns, a sexy know-it-all hero, spies, a heroine who doesn't trust the hero, meddling inlaws, even more spies, double crosses, cool computer things, and two people who can't seem to keep their hands off each other even though they know it isn't the right thing to do. Remember, it's a Harmless book, so have ice water and towels nearby.**

This book is a reissue and has been substantially changed.

A LITTLE HARMLESS REVENGE

BOOK ELEVEN

Loving someone doesn't mean you can save him from himself.

READ AN EXCERPT | BUY THE BOOK

Rumors are swirling about the fall of Sean Kaheaku, but he's ignoring them. Six months earlier, he had his entire world turned upside down and he still doesn't know what to do about it. He retreated to his home in Hawaii to recover and reassess what he wants to do now that he's been burned as a security agent.

Now lovers, Randy and Jamie arrive in Honolulu to find the lover they once knew is now even more secretive and belligerent. He refuses their help, but they are both too stubborn to leave—especially since they sense something dangerous is stalking Sean.

As the three lovers spend more time together, old feelings float to the surface and the twosome becomes a threesome. Nights are even hotter than the Hawaiian sun, and all three lovers find the connection exciting and overwhelming. But, the trouble is still out there and arrives intent on destroying Sean and everything he loves—including Randy and Jaime.

»WARNING: This book contains three spies who like to play games in and out of the bedroom, hot m/m loving, more m/m/f loving, dangerous games, lies, a few misdemeanors, and love scenes so hot, even most Addicts will be shocked. There is also a group of Alpha males with badges who will have their own series, a heroine who knows how to handle her two men, and two men who know exactly what she likes. As usual, ice and towels should be handy to help you through the book.

Formerly known as A Little Harmless Rumor. It has been substantially edited.

THE PRELUDES AND SHORTS

*S*ome stories needed a little more backstory and then there is a little fun for after the book is over.

THE PRELUDES

Prelude to a Fantasy
Prelude to a Secret
Prelude to a Revenge, Part One
Prelude to a Rumor, Part Two

THE SHORTS
Max & Anna
Chris & Cynthia
Evan & May
Micah & Dee

II

A LITTLE HARMLESS MILITARY ROMANCE

It's all Harmless, in these Harmless novellas with a military twist.

INFATUATION

BOOK ONE

To prove her love and save her man, she has to go above and beyond the call of duty.

READ AN EXCERPT | BUY THE BOOK

Francis McKade is a man in lust. He's had a crush on his best friend's little sister for years but he has never acted on it. Besides that fact that she's Malachi's sister, he's a Seal and he learned his lesson with his ex-fiancé. Women do not like being left alone for long months at a time. Still, at a wedding in Hawaii anything can happen—and does. Unfortunately, after the best night of his life, he and Mal are called away to one of their most dangerous missions.

Shannon is blown over by Kade. She's always had a crush on him and after their night together, it starts to feel a little like love. But, after the mission, Kade never calls or writes and she starts to wonder if it was all a dream. Until one night, her brother Mal drags him into her bar and grill and Shannon gets the shock of her life.

Kade isn't the man Shannon knew in Hawaii, or even the last

few years. Losing a friend and being injured changes a man, especially one who had never felt so vulnerable before. He still can't shake the terror that keeps him up at night. Worse, he is realizing that the career he loves just might be over.

Shannon is still mad, but she can't help but hurt for the man she loves. He is darker, a bit more dangerous, but beneath that, he is the Kade she's known for so many years. When he pushes her to her limits in the bedroom, Shannon refuses to back down. One way or another, this military man is going to learn there is no walking away from love—not while she still has breath in her body.

»WARNING: The following book contains: two infatuated lovers, a hard-headed military man, a determined woman, some old friends, and a little taste of New Orleans. Of course, there is a Dom who wants to be in a charge and a sub who wants to challenge him. As always, ice water is suggested while reading. It might be the first military Harmless book, but the only thing that has changed is how hot our hero looks in his uniform — not to mention out of it.

POSSESSION

BOOK TWO

Loving a military man isn't always easy and sometimes living with him is impossible.

READ AN EXCERPT | BUY THE BOOK

Deke Berg has been in love with **Sam** for ten years. From the moment they met, they could never keep their hands off each other. Their marriage was volatile and short-lived, and they were both much too young. Now, though, Deke knows what he wants in life, and Sam is at the center of his plans. Unfortunately, Sam is wary of marriage—especially to a man who broke her heart.

Sam has always loved Deke. Being a former military brat, she thought she'd been prepared for life as a military spouse. But the long separations were hard, especially dealing with the stranger who returned home. When he refused to get help, she left and always regretted it. She doesn't know if she can handle that pain again, but after spending a night together in Hawaii it's impossible for her to ignore him.

Old prejudices and painful memories aren't easy to overcome, but there is one thing Deke understands: Sam is the woman for him and he will do anything to prove his love and win her back.

»**WARNING: The following book contains: Another hard-headed military man, a woman with a wicked temper, a trip to Hawaii, one Hell Week, a few embarrassing moments, nosey brothers, and two people too stupid to realize they are perfect together. It's Harmless and military, so for your own safety make sure you have ice water nearby. The author assumes no responsibility for overheating of the reader.**

SURRENDER

BOOK THREE

To claim the woman he loves, he will have to be the Dom she desires.

READ AN EXCERPT | BUY THE BOOK

Navy Seal **Malachai Dupree** has everything a man could want. Well, not everything. The one woman he wants is too innocent for his Dominant needs, so he plays the role of supportive friend even if it kills him.

Amanda Forrester is tired of being treated as if she were fragile. She might have been through a rough patch losing her husband in the line of duty, but she is not a wimp. Her feelings for Mal have grown and she is more than ready to be the woman he needs in and out of the bedroom.

One night she pushes him too far and the result is more than either of them ever expected. Mal wants forever, but after losing one husband, commitment isn't in Amanda's vocabulary. What she doesn't realize is that Mal is one Seal who isn't backing down until he gets exactly what he wants: Amanda's total submission.

»**WARNING: The following book contains: Sexy Navy**

Seals, a stubborn woman, handcuffs and crops and all kinds of naughty things. This book has one of those hot Duprees, so you know that you will need a glass of water to cool off. Every Addict will tell you that reading a Harmless book is anything BUT harmless—so read at your own risk.

III

TASK FORCE HAWAII

EVEN PARADISE HAS A DARK SIDE

Working with local, state, and federal agencies, the men and women of TASK FORCE HAWAII work on cases ranging from bank heists to terrorism. A diverse team filled with ex-military, law enforcement, medical, and technical support, they are Hawaii's last defense against the worst criminals. The series will include six books total.

I

SEDUCTIVE REASONING

BOOK ONE

READ AN EXCERPT| BUY THE BOOK
He has a killer to catch and no time for love. Fate has other plans.

Former Army Special Forces Officer Martin "Del" Delano has enough on his hands chasing a serial killer and heading up TASK FORCE HAWAII. He definitely doesn't need the distraction of Emma Taylor. From the moment they meet, she knocks him off his feet, literally. Unfortunately, she's the best person to have on the team to make the connections to help them catch their killer.

For Emma, it's hard to ignore the lure of a man like him. Tats, muscles and his Harley cause her to have more than a few fantasies about Del. He'd never be interested in a geek like her, but she can't resist toying with him. When she pushes the teasing too far, she ends up in his bed. She convinces herself she can handle it until the moment he steals her heart.

Del can't help falling for the quirky genius. She's smart, funny and there's a sweet vulnerable side to her that only he can see. As Emma gets more involved with the investigation, she becomes the target of the psychopath. When the danger escalates, Del promises to do anything to save the woman who not only captured his heart but also his soul.

II

HOSTILE DESIRES

BOOK TWO

READ AN EXCERPT |BUY THE BOOK

As a cold case heats up, two former adversaries discover there is a thin line between love and hate.

Seven years ago, Dr. Elle Middleton's world crashed and burned. She has rebuilt her life and found comfort in her work as the medical examiner for TFH. When a new case leads to a cold case, she is beyond excited for the challenge, until she finds out the one man she wants to avoid is her partner on the case.

Graeme McGregor isn't any happier with the assignment. The doctor gets under his skin in more ways than one. He's avoided her and his attraction by keeping his distance from her, but working with her has made it impossible to resist taking a little taste.

One kiss leads to another…then to a full blown affair. But even as they draw closer to each other, secrets from that long ago murder rise to the surface. The killer's determination to stay free leads to a dangerous confrontation that puts both of their lives in peril and could leave TFH in shambles.

III

CONSTANT CRAVING

BOOK THREE

READ AN EXCERPT | BUY THE BOOK

She might trust him with her life but she's not too sure she can trust him with her heart.

Charity Edwards has never been a woman who liked to compromise–not at work and definitely not in her personal life. So, when TJ Callahan appears on the scene as their FBI liaison, she decides to take a chance on the slow talking Texan.

TJ doesn't like undercover work, but thanks to an old case, he has been tasked to do just that. He uses his position to infiltrate TFH to investigate Charity, a woman well-known for her hacking skills. His almost instant attraction he has to Charity makes it impossible not to blur the lines and he soon finds himself falling for the impossible woman.

When his assignment is revealed, Charity wants nothing to do with him, but she has no choice. Thanks to TJ's investigation, Charity's life is in jeopardy and he will do anything to protect her–even if it means sacrificing himself.

IV

TANGLED PASSIONS

BOOK FOUR

READ AN EXCERPT | BUY THE BOOK
Facing an obsessive killer proves to be easier than falling in love.

The last person Drew Franklin wants to work with is Cat Kalakau. Their history makes it difficult being in the same room, let alone being joined at the hip during a case. Months ago, they'd shared a night filled with romance and a bit more, but that ended after he was shot. Since then, even their friendship seems to have fallen apart. But he will do his job, even if spending more time with her is killing him.

Working with Drew every day reminds Cat she's to blame for his injury. It doesn't matter that she wants him more than her next breath, or that every time he looks at her she melts into a puddle of lust. She needs to resist her own desires to protect him as they hunt a serial killer targeting wealthy men signed up for dating services.

Soon though, their time together proves to be too much. One

fight leads to a kiss, which leads to so much more. Neither of them is prepared for the overwhelming need they have for each other or the connection they seem to have. But when Cat realizes Drew is the object of the killer's obsession, she will do anything to protect him even if it means sacrificing her life for his.

Made in the USA
Columbia, SC
17 May 2020